ALL NIGHT MOVIE

ALL NIGHT
MOVIE

ALICIA BORINSKY

TRANSLATED FROM THE SPANISH
BY COLA FRANZEN WITH THE AUTHOR

WITH A FOREWORD BY LUISA VALENZUELA

HYDRA BOOKS
NORTHWESTERN UNIVERSITY PRESS
EVANSTON, ILLINOIS

Hydra Books
Northwestern University Press
Evanston, Illinois 60208-4210

Copyright © 2002 by Hydra Books/Northwestern
University Press. Published 2002. All rights reserved.
Originally published in Spanish in 1997
under the title *Cine continuado*
by Ediciones Corregidor. Copyright © 1997
by Ediciones Corregidor.

Printed in the United States of America

10 9 8 7 6 5 4 3 2 1

ISBN 0-8101-1954-4

LIBRARY OF CONGRESS
CATALOGING-IN-PUBLICATION DATA
Borinsky, Alicia.
[Cine continuado. English]
All night movie / Alicia Borinsky ; translated
from the Spanish by Cola Franzen with the author ;
with a foreword by Luisa Valenzuela.
p. cm.
"Hydra books."
ISBN 0-8101-1954-4 (alk. paper)
I. Franzen, Cola. II. Title.
PQ7798.12.O687 C5613 2002
863'.64—dc21
2002010360

Contents

About Alicia Borinsky's
All Night Movie

LUISA VALENZUELA

Changing her size is the least a woman can do for love. The most would be to love, but that option is not allowed her. Because the world we enter as we open this very book is that of seduction, of suction toward a universe where the clarity of the prose reveals the darkest corners of the soul of a city that is actually the human unconscious.

And we readers completely seduced go along the edge of the precipice and at times fall on the side of laughter and at others cling for dear life to some projecting branch so as not to yield to the abyss of horror. Because horror and laughter throb together here, and the vertigo forces us to keep our eyes wide open and to travel over word after word as one chooses stones on which to wade across a river. Torrential the river, sharp-edged the stones. The way I like it. Reading in this case turns into an adventure, a safari through a jungle of highest artifice.

The writing is utterly free, and at the same time, even, measured. Nothing is set down by chance and yet chance rules here, offering us a surprise at every step.

Therein lies the seductiveness of this novel, its enchantment of eroticism clearly visible. Transgressions sprout and flourish like black tulips sprout and flourish in a telephone booth where everything happens except for a sensible call, a show of common sense.

Here we do not travel over the path of desire but the path of rituals that culminate in myth. Baudrillard would explain it better, I live, smell, touch it because this is a novel made to sharpen the five senses and awaken one more from its lethargy of centuries. The Scarred Girl lives her odyssey to arouse us, the fleet-footed followers of lowercase eva march forward to prevent by any means the apple of knowledge from falling into harmful hands. Hands worse than theirs, if such exist.

Nothing endures, everything is transformed in the contaminated universe of seduction that requires that death be within easy reach. In *All Night Movie* the discontinuity is absolute, there is no mad love without death, no possible mutation that does not leave the old skin behind glowing red hot. Bataille knew it, Alicia Borinsky puts it into action, in words that are acts of humor and violence, of brazenness, lucidity, tenderness. Love, hate. It is good to feel that such confusion succeeds and can be said, it is good to let oneself enter this farce as if immersing oneself in a bath of reality where reality surpasses itself.

All Night Movie because everything, even the most unexpected, is intertwined, because the wonderland of this Alicia when she was small was a land of darkness in which three or more pictures were shown without pause and the afternoon passed in suspense, in suspension, like a poisonous potion.

Rudolph Steiner says that poisons are gatherers of spirits. Poison flows through these pages under the disconcerting disguise of hearts of palm trees, contaminating hearts of palms just as they contaminate the hearts of the characters. Nothing endures, everything is transformed, someone changes size. It is not Alicia: Alicia does not drink the potion, through the marvelous mediation of writing she passes it on to her heroine the Invisible Woman/Felipa/Matilde/Laura/Juana/the doll. One and the same person in her diverse avatars, the giantess and the midget, the one who unfolds and the one who is many, murderess and executioner. Alicia (Borinsky) only watches her from her place barely grazed by a fleeting first person as she gives her a flick and moves her onto something else.

The potion will be drunk by us readers, caught in the subtle and slippery net of a writing that dances, that gives off sparks of purpurin, blinding at times. Now and then tango lyrics like touchstones will keep pointing the way out of the cave. Or the way deeper in, to drink the cup down to the lees, still wanting more, more threats and more jokes, corruptions, and disguises. We endorse it all, accept the challenge. The reward does not consist in the suspension of disbelief. It consists in another belief that will open wide the doors for us to go out and play.

ALL NIGHT MOVIE

READER:
LET'S GET ALL DRESSED UP
AND GO TO THE MOVIES.
(I'LL GROPE YOU IN THE DARK
BUT YOU'LL NEED
A LOT OF LUCK
BECAUSE THE UPS AND DOWNS
OF THIS NOVEL,
LIKE MY LOVE,
ARE A BANANA PEEL, A THORN,
AND A NONSTOP FASHION SHOW.)

I

Her story told by me,
not even eyewitness
Sad but good for dancing

She says good-bye in black and white

You'll say it's outrageous it can't be that she walks free after such a light sentence after such a pleasant stay in a cute little cell with air conditioning, a garden in front and view of the lake. It's the kind of thing I overheard in the warm air of the siesta when I came out of the bathroom, and we women would see as the very truth of our lives. You danced, my dear neighbors, danced eyes bulging and hair hidden by a kerchief. It's not just words. It's a blast, a pleasure and now she, poking fun at our deepest hopes, admits it and says: I'm happy because I'm leaving. I'm moving. Going off to another neighborhood. Alone. She could feel every single sound, the fury and disgust they had for her because she said it: I'm leaving.

Bye. Bag in hand. You want to come with me to the station? Now you I'm going to miss. Want to come along? Carry this bag for me, it's not too heavy, my darling. After all, I wouldn't want you to get a hernia on my account. And then you laughed because you found it funny the idea that I might get a hernia or maybe because you were thinking of one of the nurses in the hospital, in those starched uniforms that twenty years later would weave through my destiny day and night. Maybe you already knew about the accident and then you laughed because why do anything else. Fine, let's go, kid, if we say good-bye like in the movies, don't make me wait.

I followed close behind you, almost out of breath, guessing that you were sweating beneath those nylon stockings, my intuition telling me that a little higher up you were gradually getting wet from enthusiasm. I followed you closely, mean hot bitch, letting me go off to school like a sick puppy so that I'd think of how you looked at my classmates. Later I followed you from a distance and tried to keep out of sight but we were living in the same neighborhood with insolently new trees and too much sun and you saw me. Come on, we don't have too much time. When the train arrived you said to me: I'm not leaving you my telephone number. And I'm not leaving you my address because I'm going to make a new life for myself but I wish you lots of luck, enjoy yourself, hope you have many sweethearts, don't forget your divorced neighbor who taught you so much and then didn't whisk you away. I held your cheeks and in front of everybody gave you a kiss, I know you felt my tongue and know you liked it because you whispered in my ear baby girl, sweetie, mummy's little pet.

The world moves fast and in straight lines when you go by train. There were businesses, small shops built by their owners with plastic knickknacks and cheap jewelry for sale, fruit and vegetable stands, and stores reeking of salami and cheese. The seasons were changing and when they reached the city it was already winter, she had to put on her fur coat, as for her nail polish, it was chipped, her garter belt stretched and if I'd been looking at her I would have guessed the rolls of fat already gathering around the waist. But she was walking alone now along a street lit up by signs that said GIRLS A THOUSAND GIRLS HUMAN SAUSAGE DANCING COCA-COLA THE BE-WITCHED PANTHER she was walking alone because she was looking for trouble walking alone looking for action and needed money   walking alone but she wasn't yet because for that she needed to be independent   she needed a nice bank account without a mortgage without fees for this and that. It was a different time and she was parading herself like someone on the lookout for business but nobody came near her. *The Invisible Woman,* she said to herself. She was invisible because for the others yes, of course, men came up to them wearing anonymous disguises, jackets smelling vaguely of cologne and cigarettes, gray trousers, wrinkled at the fly from anticipation, with one or another spot already foretelling the future failure. To the other women yes but to her no. No matter how wide she opened her coat to show off her body. No matter how much she swiveled her hips to say I'm in the market.

May I help you, miss? What would you like? When he bent over to write TEQUILA WITH A DROP OF WARM LEMON JUICE IN A TALL CHILLED GLASS she took his hand while moving her big toe up his leg all the way to the groin, grazing the rough gray serge pants. He reached down, grabbed the sole of her right foot, and delivered a message: At the exit there is a telephone booth with a seat and if you know what's coming you'll wait for me there until I show up but you'll have to be patient, get some cash together because my lessons do not come cheap. He said all this without moving his lips. She knew it. She was good at these things and besides there were some clues such as the unmistakable trickle of saliva coming down the left corner of his mouth.

His name was Felipe. She saw it on the ID bracelet he wore around his hairy wrist. And you, miss, what do they call you?

What's it to you? Are you going to ask me for a date? Or maybe you want to see if I'm in the directory?

He didn't hesitate even a second. He hit her so hard with his gloved hand that she fell at his feet and then heard the question clearly. What's your name, bitch? As she answered she felt a kind of intoxication, unknown new shivers running through her body urging her to learn, be a good girl, do a complicated tango step in which she would pull up her bent legs to give birth to a smiling crocodile. FELIPA and she was happy beyond measure. Now she licked his shoes, her stomach singing with street dirt, a bitter taste of grass blades and discarded paper wrappers. FELIPA at your service, sir. He crouched down and stroked her ass, stuck a finger inside that suddenly seemed to grow longer while she said more more yes deeper and with his free hand covered her face with something soft, smelly, vaguely familiar. FELIPA FELIPA at your service sir she said time and again as her fine airs turned into sighs, throbs so he would say I'll give it to you out of pity you shit, you nobody filthy bitch she wasted no time unbuttoned, stepped out of her clothes, and crouched naked in the telephone booth out of sight from passersby she insisted please please because, screaming at the top of her voice, she realized that now finally she had started something. The long road was about to open.

Each time she went into this telephone booth wearing sandals she could feel the caress of the black fleshy tulips that grew on the floor and the walls. There was something in the booth, a whiff, that changed people's conversations. Without anybody noticing, voices were lowered. Women fondled their breasts as they talked to their mothers, the most pious teenage girls told their sweethearts about certain nocturnal yearnings and suggested meetings in daring locations abuzz with drug deals and child prostitution; some boys would turn up scared but excited only to find that the girls had not come because, their hearts pounding, they crossed themselves as soon as they left the booth and were cleansed by the air of the square; traveling salesmen interrupted the driest business deals to suggest blackmail schemes for imaginary rapes with much clicking of tongues and lewd enticements; some rejected the offers but many got into the game creating a real lottery that changed the nature of business in vast parts of the city.

For Felipa, heart beating with wisdom, the booth was a nuptial chamber. With each Felipe she lured in, her body got better attuned to the corners, the uneven surfaces, and the distance between the receiver and her back. After several months of practice with the waiter she gained a skill but lost a passion.

She's in an empty room. The voile curtains let in light and a sea breeze that worked its way into her armpits. She's happy. She can measure it, prove it with every inch of the white wall and now she will close her eyes so she won't see who is coming near her, smelling of tanning lotion and iodine. She doesn't want to see him because she stretches out her hand and now feels the sand stuck to his skin, at a touch she knows he's been in the sun, his skin is warm, tight and then she has to massage it so he'll be grateful and will give her what she's after. Matilde, I've brought you the orchids you asked me for. And here's your manzanilla tea. I won't put it down because I want to serve it to you myself. Sip by sip, dear darling Matilde. Apple of my eye. Let's see, open your lips, let me see your beautiful rosy palate. I'll make you well again.

The music begins almost immediately. You can hear kettle-drums among the palms, tinkling of cocktail spoons in crystal glasses. And then he says to her: Matías, for you I will always be Matías. They dance with eyes closed. His curly eyelashes tickled Matilde's cheeks. She feels he pulls away because he's a man and wants to keep his passion in check out of respect but she pursues him, presses near insistent, says don't be ashamed it's only a dance but he repeats I want to get married have kids send them to school, cook seafood casserole every day for you. She has taken off her clothes. She's dancing before him while he pulls out a marriage contract and asks her to sign it but she lets him smell her perfume, grope her, wants him to forget it and just when he's about to put the contract away the tele-phone rings.

She hadn't gone crazy but was getting close. In the mornings she brushed her teeth and attended a temple of a vague reli-gious sect where she met with women wearing dark skirts and gray blouses and little knitted wool jackets in contrasting col-ors. They talked in hushed voices before prostrating them-selves at an altar where they'd placed offerings of food and em-broideries. They always left before the chorus of girls aban-doned by their aunts arrived. They didn't like the spectacle. They weren't interested in the emotion of the moment when they sang of their misfortunes screaming in loud voices so that Felipa Matilde would give them the signal and they could rush to eat and offer the apples that the women had brought. They played Eve, girls in paradise, but they knew they were in a neighborhood fueled by illusions of smuggling, tax evasion, and discreet muggings done with gloved hands. The girls adored her. They recognized her every time despite the disguises and although she'd not yet given them anything, they did compute and hatch plans for their life savings that would not include charity since this was a realistic cult, based on observation of human nature and not on the imagination of some half-crazed eccentric visionary.

Inside Matilde Felipa stopped being herself to play with them at Eve and the apple; they became drunk with guilt, did a dance shot through by gasps, rapid changes of rhythm that left them breathless, on the floor, sweaty, lying over the chest of a companion who sometimes insisted on easing the fatigue with a slow repertory of caresses. They were her bunnies, baby girls, but also her judges and heiresses. Matilde kept her duties in the telephone booth a secret because by that time she had already learned it was better not to speak about certain things and when she went out wearing her reversible coat, the fur hidden inside, modest brown side on view, she would say: I'm going to buy cookies or I have an appointment with the dentist or they're waiting for me this minute at the consulate. That last was to prepare an eventual change of booth because the bribes she had to give the police so they'd let her keep up with her activities had shot up due to the economic crisis that had now spread throughout the country.

What to do with her mail?
It really gets to her
She decides to act but above all read it

Dear daughter,

I've been expecting you for many years. Your letter was a surprise because I thought that by now you'd forgotten all about me and the family that always remembers you. It's not that we don't want to see you but this is a difficult moment for us, some unexpected expenses have left us with few resources, so with a very sorrowful heart, my dearest daughter, I have to tell you that we cannot send you the ticket you ask for. Perhaps you can save a little money from your job as telephone operator, perhaps I can get a little extra somewhere, and after some years we'll have a sufficient amount. We pray that you are enjoying good health at the moment. With a loving embrace, your mama who never forgets you.

Occupant of telephone booth No. 6758B:

We hereby notify you that the space that you have been occupying illegally since the month of March of the present year must be vacated at the date of receipt of this warning under penalty of incarceration and the payment of a fine of 1,000 pesos per day starting from the date of this official warning.

Lic. Raimundo Massotti
Deputy Director
Department of Public Morals and Telecommunications

Dear consumer:

We regret to inform you that we can no longer continue to provide you with the 20 mm. weekly dosage of Fontamil you have ordered and prepaid due to the present ban of its sale to the public. If you wish to retrieve your deposit, please come in person during the next 90 days to the office where the original order was placed. If

the refund due you is not claimed within the stated time period, the monies will become the property of our company.

Yrs. truly,
Rosamaría Campodónico
General Director

She was sure. She could bet her life on it. That Rosamaría and that Raimundo must know one another and are out there somewhere making fun of her. They're in a secluded place, in a small restaurant with violin music, she would order pheasant stuffed with nuts and raisins while he would extol the virtues of the duck with orange sauce. But please, what bad taste. To act so mean toward a divorced woman who had moved into a telephone booth. Be so mean for no reason because what could it matter to them that she threw out people who wanted to make telephone calls if there are so many other booths in the city, if not exactly on that corner. The black tulips, that must be it. Jealous that they should breathe and flutter with no earth whatsoever. No understanding of that garden that came out of the metal and hard rubber of the telephone, filtered through the holes of the speaker, and caressed the ears of the users. She tended her garden with words and gestures, aided by clients who now had passwords:

Operator
   Operator
May I please make a brief call? How much for the first ten minutes?

LONG DISTANCE, EVERYTHING INCLUDED, FIFTY FOR A HALF HOUR. LOCAL, TEN MINUTES THIRTY OR TWENTY-FIVE DEPENDING ON THE AGE.

said the sign she showed them with a wink. She was a charmer. Had an enterprising spirit and that's why all this makes us so sad that she's more in the street than before, poor woman, thrown completely on her own without a protector to take charge of things. But let's not get upset. She had resources. She hadn't forgotten the place where she'd deposited her savings had not blown her money on trinkets. She is, despite appearances, a modern woman up to the challenge of her circumstances. She walks and walks first of all to find pen paper and stamps:

My dear dear mama,

I don't need a ticket but I could use a nice warm bed to protect me from the winter and my poor health. You don't have to provide my food but I would like you to invite me for some empanadas like the ones you used to make on Sundays after the game. I'll see you as soon as you let me know you've received this letter and my room has been redecorated.

I love you, your daughter
Estela Ramona del Carpio

Dear Bochîta,

Your father's death left us almost bankrupt. I had to make do as well as I could and now that you know the truth you won't be surprised when I tell you I found myself in the position of having to rent rooms. The house has been converted into a pensión. *I fixed up a place for myself in the basement and there with my futon and a heater I spend my days coming and going with work I do for the residents. They're all nice people, one is a teacher, there's a bank employee, and a dancer. If you're not disgusted by the idea, I can offer you a corner of the basement. We can put in a futon and until you find something better you could keep me company, help with the*

16

chores. How nice it would be if you came back in time for the picnic on the first day of spring! I know this news may make you feel very sad but I didn't want to keep hiding the truth of my situation from you.

As always, your mama

Dearest ones! THE LAW!

Raquel comes noiselessly into the bar. She carries a wine-colored leather briefcase, wears heels, skirt with a slit that comes to just above her knee, and a green wool jacket with gold-zippered pockets; on the left side one can see the tip of a thin red-dyed snakeskin whip.

—I've come to check on neighbors' complaints. They say prostitutes' services are sold from here.

—Miss, you are very mistaken. This is a decent bar. Pastries. Sherry. Vermouth. Cheese. Olives. Peanuts. Raw ham and salami snacks. Red wine. A bar. We even had codfish for the Spaniards who will not give it up. Although I bet they know how bad it is for you.

—Give me a glass of red wine and start singing because I don't have much time.

—What do you want me to sing? Ask me anything of Caruso because I'm a learned man and know all the classical repertory. I mean the one of the artists of the past. Because now they're all corrupt. What can I tell you. It's not worthwhile even to listen to them on the radio. Money, money, and more money is the sound that comes from their chest. I want money they sing because now there's nothing of art left. Just a deal here, another there, this one got me to sing at La Scala, the other arranged a concert at Carnegie Hall, they'll go to Manaus, the Colón, San Isidro, Bangladesh, it doesn't matter. Today, baby, it's all about money. Myself look I appreciate you so much that this wine I serve you is on the house so you'll see I'm not like the others. A decent guy. You won't see many like me. I like your classy looks. Do you always dress like this? Those heels must be extremely uncomfortable but they give people ideas, they go to the head and make you dizzy and that little whip, my God. For a few minutes of punishment I'll give you the entire repertory of Agustín Lara and Sinatra together because I like you, I find you irresistible, I smell elegance, virtue, hard work, honesty.

19

—Look, stop clowning around I'm here to conduct an investigation. You know very well what I mean. Don't play dumb with me because I'm here to satisfy the desire for justice on the part of people with children, concerned for the moral well-being of the community, worried that a handful of perverts might ruin their future, the investment in their homes and screw up their whole lives.

—The problem with you is you talk too much. That little whip tells me everything. It chafes. You have an itch but don't want to admit it. You want to make a telephone call but don't want to get into a mess.

—Telephone calls. That's exactly what I've come to talk to you about.

—Sit down and I'll explain. That's it. Cross your legs so I don't get ideas before I finish telling you a story you're going to find very interesting. I want to see you wield that little whip of yours with those long fingers and scarlet nails.

She gets ready to return
but doesn't know it
(let's watch her with pity
please don't heckle)

Matilde Felipa is feeling sad. All of a sudden she looks like a stray dog. *Fucking sick bitch* the last one who'd passed through the telephone booth said to her before asking her to give him his money back. Sick bitch but not stupid so she bit him hard to make him leave, screaming, humiliated, doubled over, swearing she'd pay for what she'd done. She'd counted her money listlessly. She missed her medicine. She missed her resentment. She'd forgotten the sorrows she had to purge. She'd completed her mission and now doesn't understand why she'd ever moved into the booth in the first place. The neon lights had stopped blinking coded messages. My dears, she'll fade on us like the tulips. She'll keep wilting, bitter disillusioned flower.

—May I, miss?

—Yes, I was just going.

—Look, I don't want to cut in. If you have to make a call, please go ahead, I'll wait. The person expecting my call will wait as long as needed.

—No, no. Don't mention it.

The man who was going to change her life, cause her to recognize streets she'd only glimpsed in dreams and to dress herself in evening gowns every night according to his whims, had dirty nails and wore shoes with thick heels to make him seem taller, but even so she was still a head higher than he was. As a baby he'd had curly hair, he would tell her some months later, the fourth of June, day of his fiftieth birthday.

—Hi, Lucía, I miss you with all my heart. I've been unable to sleep thinking of you night and day. Nobody like you. I'd see you come out of the shower, with your hair shiny black after the shampoo I gave you and I thought of how I'd massage you nice and slow pausing over those wonderfully warm parts of your body that drive me crazy.

When he got to that part he moved his jaws as if he wanted to swallow something and a tear sprang out from so much emotion. Then he promised endless love, stroked the tulips, rubbed his neck, unbuttoned his shirt revealing his bushy chest said he could stand it no longer. That's the way it was for three weeks while Matilde Felipa waited her turn because by then she'd developed a keen interest in her mama's boarders and kept up long conversations about their most intimate habits and the best ways to save money on the cost of food for the *pensión,* you couldn't be too careful these days with prices shooting sky high. The tale of love he told in the telephone booth filled her with envy. She imagined Lucía coming out of the shower, went over her body with a teenager's curiosity, dreamed of buying earrings to surprise her. Alone in front of the mirror she passed a fingér over her lips believing herself to be her, in ecstasy while he massaged her, making her turn this way and that, molding her body for pleasure. Matilde Felipa sighed, waited in line, and pretended to count the sparrows on the limb of the tree growing apathetically on the left side of the booth beside the kiosk with magazines and newspapers where she had not noticed the announcements of a new campaign for morality and good behavior.

His name was Pascual Domenico Fracci. He had five sons, all accountants, upright, good citizens with political opinions regarding the proper direction of the local government, ready to be active in the PTA when their own children reached school age, good men concerned about the future of the community. That's why, when the last one was ready to establish a household, get married, buy toothpaste in the large economy size, he decided it was the right moment to leave that life and take off. His wife hardly noticed his absence because during the past twenty years of their marriage he'd spent the greater part of his time in the family business, a store that made quite a bit of money from the sale of vaguely useful or decorative objects that he wrapped carefully in colored paper and an adhesive tape that came apart the minute the customer took it in his hands. It would be very wrong to say that he thought things through. He had only desires left, he acted on impulse. He realized it when he began to spy on what was going on in the telephone booth and wove a fantastic plan that would remove him once and for all from that existence so tenuous, so without rhyme or reason.

—I want to take care of you, Lucía, love of my life, I want you to think of nobody but me day and night. I want to pamper you. Make you feel safe. At night I'll cuddle you in my arms, sing you lullabies while my hands wander over those places I know so well.

In the booth even the tulips were changing color, black no longer suited them, now they were tinted a nuptial rose, they swayed, the petals grazing each other with an almost catlike purr, a summery luminous sound. Matilde Felipa had grown smaller. Timidity and desire had seeped into her body and almost without realizing it the very idea of Lucía had transformed her. She was now a woman of short stature, chubby, with ankles slightly swollen, flabby muscles, in need of a massage. He, out of the corner of his eye, recognized that she'd been losing her arrogance of the first days and continued to apply the treatment that now went on days and nights: he gave her recipes for getting rid of malaria, nits, for preparing a vegetarian stew, also guitar classes and moments of great erotic inspiration alluding to patriotic holidays. Pascual Domenico was patient. The years of conjugal servitude had prepared him well. He could wait and keep on waiting. This time he didn't want to leave anything unfinished. He knew that Matilde Felipa had not yet reached his exact size and continued with his harangues until one evening when a bus strike had left the stores vacant and there were signs of a rainy autumn, he looked her straight in the eyes and, seeing that she was blushing, knew she was ready to give the right answer.

—Tell me, cutie pie, what's your name?

—Lucía, sir.

She said it. Red-faced. Surprised by his insolence. With sweaty palms the ring from First Communion slipped off her finger in a slippery, inexorable fall. She saw it disappear in the gutter atop a yellow ribbon with the name of the bakery on the corner in red letters ORTIZ BAKERY, and her stomach sang in anticipation of the cream pastries they'd eat twenty minutes later, squeezing them in their hands, letting the cream seep between the fingers before mingling with the amorous fluids that now yes were frankly unleashed because they knew they were united by a joke much stronger than any adversity.

He was the way you've imagined him, you told me one afternoon years later. I wanted you to recognize me for more than my name, remember our farewell and our games but you persisted in talking to me of your great love, of the incredible reduction of your height that had minimized you so you might arise hot and true every night, and every evening as the wife of Pascual Domenico.

He beat the hell out of you and later the two of you hot, he would eat you up, kiss you, console you, ask forgiveness and say: Baby I'll buy you some chocolates

take you for a walk

we'll have a sunny apartment

I'll sing you songs in French

and he dedicated Italian melodies to you with tearfully sad lyrics that spoke of voyages on ships that never returned, fiery sunsets during which two lovers gazing into each others' eyes suddenly understand that this will be their last meeting and you, so he wouldn't be disillusioned, would say:

French is such a romantic language

I like the way you sing it and pronounce it so clearly

silly foolish baby doll

Pascual Domenico repeated over and over and lifting you high in the air carried you around in his arms, mussed your hair, undressed you, called you Lucía.

We miss her because she was so cute

The girls of the Eva cult began to march through the neighborhood carrying apples in their hands. At first the neighbors thought they were farm girls and some wanted to buy fruit. *Two and a half kilos for me of the red ones. No, better mix them with the green, although now they're a bit tart, give me four yellow ones. But, what are you doing? Are you crazy? Why spit at me?*

They're not selling anything. They're not farm girls or artists or beggars or demonstrators they have no cause.

Nothing matters to them.

They ask no favors.

They show their apples and laugh among themselves. Exchange glances. Make remarks, murmur, whisper. Plot. **Plot.** It's believed in the neighborhood and in the rest of the city that they are plotting something because this is a mistrustful country, a country of traitors, cuckolds, and hopeless types who cannot recognize the weirdness in the girls' eyes and that they walk as if wounded because of the absence of the black tulips and the high heels. They look and look for her, need her, long for her brazen breath, the suspicion of her plans, the tinkle of coins in her pockets, and the insolence of her hips before possible clients. The girls of the Eva cult want to see her again in the telephone booth, guess at her earnings. They're concerned, anxious and don't know, don't understand, blinded by nostalgia.

their methods are wrong

their tactics are from a bygone era

ignorant bloodhounds

misty-eyed romantics

Raquel also wanted to find her to take a statement. The activity in the booth that gave rise to the protests had ended. The tulips, faded, feeble, lay on the floor among discarded cigarette butts and rumpled pieces of paper their telephone numbers erased from being stepped on so much. But now you will have guessed. Other women, following her example, are doing the same thing. They are crude, noisy, dye their hair, discuss the

27

price in a loud voice. They wait in doorways to kneel before men who open raincoats smelling of dampness and show them a source of income, a modest arrow, a silent story they have no interest in testing.

Any woman with a little whip wants to use it sometime or other. Above all if it's red. Raquel is no exception. In the riot of caresses, frictions, and business deals she found her prey, the back on which she would discharge her fury. She didn't even know her name but she really needed to meet that woman. Neighbors, the waiters in the bar, the teenagers who lined up to talk to their sweethearts, could tell her little. The girls of the cult, the odd ones, the ones without rhyme or reason, the ones with the apples, the ones thrown out of paradise, would take her to their patron and then she would unleash her fury, demonstrate the power of her whip, would say to her

intruder,

faker,

this is the spirit of the law.

She infiltrated the girls' marches. Made friends with them through tricks and flattery, gave them a recipe for covering the apples with wax so they wouldn't rot and would shine forever. That's how the fragrance of their marches ended, the apples turned hard, and one day, their charm gone, they vanished and were replaced by a red banner. Let's embroider the face of our patron on it, Raquel suggested. We'll make a picture that will identify her. Something that allows us to locate her. No, no, and no, they answered, not that kind of search, you don't understand us yet. Our patron is a woman like no other. She only resembles herself.

Homes that kill

Worried, panting. She runs along the same streets that saw her arrive, passes the girls of the cult who don't recognize her and almost step on her, overtakes Raquel, stumbles over the point of the whip making it fall but she doesn't stop to pick it up because she's in a hurry and also on the run. Under her arm she's carrying the little stool she needs to be able to reach the mouthpiece of the public telephone. Do I have enough money? Will she be at home?

—Mama? How lucky to find you at home. Get everything ready.

—Yes, in the basement, I'll manage anywhere. No, don't tell anyone I'm coming, leave the back door open.

—No, don't go to the station.

—That's not the reason, but nobody, nobody must know that I'm coming back.

—Not even her.

—Yes, certainly I want to see you, but we have to be careful.

—Mama, are you paying close attention? You have to keep my secret. I just killed a man.

II
Downtown glitter

Vacant eyes. Distracted she walked along. From time to time she leaned over to pick up a coin or a piece of paper and her face lit up for a few seconds but once she put her find into one of the many plastic bags she carried hanging from both arms she became an ambulatory statue once again, an impassive woman. Rosa hung out in an alley that bordered on a building that had been a theater for variety shows twenty years earlier. Time had upset the symmetry of two useless balconies, now only a roost for pigeons and dumping place for trash scattered by the wind. A small group of people defied the pigeon shit to attend lively religious services there on Thursdays and Sundays. They were so few of them they greeted each other at the entrance with oversolemn handshakes for this neighborhood grown dull and gray due to the economic crisis and the community's aesthetic indifference.

The girls of the Eva cult couldn't stand the shabby surroundings. They were young. Wore miniskirts. Showed a lot of attitude. Some could still smell the fiery fragrance of the lost apple. They perceived what everybody had forgotten; the spirit of chorus girls with proud legs and pointed breasts was alive in them. Rosa didn't notice them at first because she was always asleep when they arrived, she faked she was drunk so nobody would be frightened by the visions of her extreme lucidity.

Raquel saw her right away because she had the nose of a bloodhound. Sprawled out, eyes closed and an empty rum bottle beside her, Rosa was, without doubt, the ideal accomplice. *She has nothing to lose, not even a passport so she can take off abroad, not even a miserable little salary from a lousy job so she can be poor but dignified, in less than half an hour I'll be her soulmate, the lost link of her will to live,* Raquel said to herself while caressing the red whip because she was getting a callus on her finger from stroking the plaited leather.

The girls of the cult had forgotten that Raquel was a recent arrival. After all, they had no time for intimacies and if they did, they'd use it for more interesting things, for instance, to strike up conversations with one of the bunch of boys who courted them with great hopes.

—I'll dress you in party clothes, get you a total makeover, take you to the hairdresser's, the fragrance boutique, and in less than a day nobody will know the difference. They'll adore you and together we'll take over the movement

      they'll photograph us as we come out from premieres

          we'll be asked to the openings of the most important buildings

              I'll give you all the rum you need then but not now because we have to be on guard, companion, dear friend, leader.

That's how she was talking to Rosa thinking she was asleep. She chose different words and situations to impress her but the tune was always the same: success, fame, a dramatic change of social class. Rosa kept up the pretense of sleeping because this wasn't the first time a passerby had approached her with vague proposals of collaborations related to some ad campaign or, most often, some magic pill or another. One day when it was raining Raquel slipped on something greasy, a mix of banana peel and used condom and fell on top of Rosa before beginning her harangue. Rosa opened her eyes, and meeting for the first time Raquel's feline gaze, felt her apathy ebb away.

—What if we both take part in the church contest. I'm going.

—What contest?

—The bicycle race. They have it every year and I've never had the nerve to enter because you need a partner, but it would be a good way to see if we can work together.

—I don't know, if we lose my plan goes to hell before I even tell you what it is. Frankly, it doesn't seem very practical to me, boring. Because, what use is a contest? It's tempting luck, putting yourself out so someone can play games with you, make you turn somersaults. I'd rather plan everything in a professional way, be in the forefront of circumstances. We could bribe the nuns so they'll give us the prize, now that really appeals to me. Rosa was already yawning from boredom that came from the time her hands would turn purple from the bleach she used for the laundry.

—Come on, you're going to enjoy it.

—I don't need a makeover. That's only for fags. We women no longer care about such things anymore.

Muñequita linda / my own little Goldilocks

High heels were the only thing she couldn't wear. She had corns. Calluses. Hitting the pavement made her feet into crags. That's why when you looked at her you got a jolt going from the fitted Chanel suit to clunky black shoes. Raquel spoiled her, called her little tennis racquet, hummingbird, Goldilocks, but she was licking her chops now thinking of how she could make her shut up the minute she felt the whip.

They went to a restaurant but the staff didn't want to serve them because such a close friendship embarrassed them, that and so much smell of talcum powder but in the bar they were given a special table beside the orchestra and were even brought BLTs to calm their hunger along with two warm beers because Rosa had acquired a taste for recycled stuff.

—How is it you believed the business of the church contest? What made you swallow any stupid thing I told you? I never thought you'd fall into that trap. But what can I say, that's life. What goes around comes around and sometimes in spades. And here we are.

She was boasting. With the toothpick moving in the left corner of her lip like a little animal about to take flight, and expressive hands, a bit shiny because of the constant sweat that soaked her every hour and a half since she caught a grotesque disease, no doubt incubated for years before showing any symptoms but it didn't matter all that much because she'd never kissed anybody on the mouth. Disgust. Lack of opportunity. Distracted by other parts of the body, more fragrant openings, bushier surfaces. When they heard the first tango they didn't hesitate one minute. They got up. They became one, glued by sweat and the desire to show off.

Raquel hid the pain caused by the toothpick when it jammed into her cheek. She took deep breaths while the other one belched and enveloped her in a smell of beer and olives. She put up with it long enough for them to realize that nobody was

36

interested in what they were doing because a fourteen-year-old girl dressed like a choirgirl was doing a complicated striptease that lasted all night.

The girl's clothes taken off in reverse order were:

jacket with gold border, plastic pockets

checked skirt of a shiny material, perhaps aluminum foil

cashmere sweater

cotton sweater

Girl Scout blouse

T-shirt with logo of the losing soccer team that left the entire country sunk in the deepest sadness

loose pants

tight pants

panties stolen from a transvestite when he changed them for a Hawaiian skirt in the ladies room of a restaurant famous for the quality of the disinfectant they put on the mirrors

long transparent stockings with a design resembling lace (gray tones)

satin bra with a little fleur-de-lis on each nipple

a diaper

a sanitary napkin

a diaphragm

(because, you've all guessed, her nudity was absolute and the public valued her concentration day after day)

WHAT IS IT TO THEM A COMMON ORDINARY COUPLE TWO CHEAP PERVERTED WOMEN DANCING A TANGO

Such things made no impression, they were out of place since they'd sent all abnormal types to the circus. The people were curious but not naive. Eager for things on a higher plane, to get to the heart of the matter, that stirred them, yes, and the girl, well, the girl was something else. From her one could learn without homework. She was truly there. No need for panting or dramatic moves. So she stole the show and the other two women, satisfied, somewhat dizzy from the rhythm they'd discovered together, sat down to rest and to share in the great sight of Noemí, star student, slowly stripping off layer after layer.

Dear Diary,

Today I got almost no tips. Either they were so entranced they forgot. Or they are just leeches who expect freebies. The women who were dancing the tango took me out to eat. If it hadn't been for them, I would've gone hungry. Now it makes two nights I've gone out with them. Could they want something from me?

I tried to call you
but the line was always busy

Mama had made spaghetti with tomato sauce and meatballs.

She'd taken the rollers out of her hair and now sported a mane of wiry curls.

We know she's posing for the photo that the boarder from room 5 will take of them just as soon as the girl comes into the room.

She's arrived, agitated with clothes straight from the cleaners. Tall, thin, figure like Greta Garbo: broad shoulders, very thin lips, gray raincoat.

She's arrived and the mama realizes that it's her daughter from her applesauce breath. I tell you once you have it you can't get rid of it no matter how much you spend on mints and lipstick. They embrace, kiss each other, but for now there won't be much to say, that will only come later when she abandons her transvestite elegance under the shower and confesses to the crime as she files those nails of hers that keep turning red without any need for polish.

I'd like to but we have to think about the others

(we did what we had to do and other things that she
told and were told to her and let's skip over this part
so that you and I can whisper our own little secrets to
each other best to do it at sunset or in the moonlight if
we can't make it to the sauna and there really go to
work taking stock of our vaginas, the smoothness of
our legs, the front and back of our stories)

She dances. At last!

The girl showed up. Ready for her number. The audience was larger than usual.

Dapper high school teachers with dandruff flakes on their blue sailor blazers.

Women fragrant with products.

Plastic surgeons alert to each detail of her body in order to reproduce it in the flabby well-heeled women who bankrolled vacations to places where they sell electronic gadgets, polyester tablecloths, and condoms made of thin soft materials that are oh so wonderful and then there's no more need for sassy lovers with prurient morals and psychological peculiarities.

A nun with dark glasses and scandalous underclothes who at the most unexpected moment will leap forward throw caution to the wind and confess a hopeless love to her.

The girl is dancing now for everybody but most of all for her diary because she knows that to keep on writing she'll have to have an adventure but how and where if this tiring striptease only allows her to collect a few coins and count them without even enough time to buy a lollipop, a condom, or a poster of the girls of the Eva cult licking apples with scandalously red tongues, almost hairy.

anybody can have an accident

—So you killed a man. I can't believe it. You were always so very quiet. Obviously now you've changed completely, with that imposing look. Odd to grow after your first period. I always thought that a girl stayed at the same height she was at the time her monthlies started. A little red trickle and that's it. You can get pregnant, but forget about growing. You on the other hand.

—I killed him but it looked like an accident.

—Poison. You gave him cyanide. You put sedatives in a shot of vodka and later you served him yogurt two years out of date. You gave him fermented wine with canapes of hearts of palm canned in a gloomy plant where the people sweat and sing songs in a Guarani so limpid and musical there are no words and no safeguards against botulism. So many ways. I've always said poisoning is the most fitting method for the submissive nature of women, servants, cooks. It gives a woman the chance to take care of the sick person. Clean up the vomit and increase the dosage while he thanks us with tears in his eyes and begs us not to abandon him because he's afraid of the nurse who by this time is already fed up with the things that happen in the house, family rows, in this fucking country where you never know what may happen tomorrow.

—You talk as if you'd done it yourself.

—You're mature enough to understand me now that you wear a raincoat. That was the main thing that made me realize that I was face to face with a grown-up daughter, an adult. A woman who wears a raincoat is somebody to be reckoned with. Not a sweet little thing type who jumps into a taxi at the first drop of rain. And a gray one, you get it? Nothing colored, gray, to hide spots, experiences, all that. Imagine, I've always found a certain something about you because the deceased insisted so much in giving you a traditional education it seemed to me you were never going to be able to free yourself from it but

46

your divorce and that girl that came looking for you with such anxiety began to convince me that . . .

—A girl?

—Yes, she said you'd been neighbors, that she admired you so much, something about having gone with you to the train, and so on now I forget, it was just when the business of the deceased well, obviously, at that time he was ill and I had no resources, not like now. Bochita, all in all, my life is more interesting in the *pensión*. You've not yet seen what it's like on a day when there's a general strike. I make a stew and we all sit around the table and talk about times gone by. Naturally, I listen without saying a word because I have to keep my dignity as lady of the house but I find out what's going on with them and I see every little thing so it would take me a lifetime to tell you because the truth is with the boarders and all I have less work now than when I was alone with the deceased who with one whim or another, particularly toward the end with that business of the stomach troubles that required so much attention. Four nurses passed through here and every one agreed: You, señora, are a saint. One of them was my first boarder.

—You never told me what happened to my dad, what gave him those dizzy spells.

—What can I tell you. A case of indigestion. I would say something in the meatballs. Or maybe that pizza he loved to eat from the place on the corner.

—Strange that it didn't seem to bother you.

—For heaven's sake, weren't you going to tell me how you did it?

47

I am nothing without you

Dear Diary:

The señoras have their whims. Today they examined me from head to foot to find out how I can wear so many clothes and still look so slender. They took me to a clinic to have X rays made. They want to know me better but don't trust what I say. They've been lied to a lot in life. They're looking for something. They're looking for someone and want me to help them. I'll do it, dear diary, I'll be their bloodhound not because they pay me but because at bottom I'd also like to know who this eva is and perhaps we'll run across her trail. Dear diary, what can I get out of it? What clothes or what body hair so they'll call me dear friend, *amiguita,* stop looking at me with that suspicious air and let me laugh at their jokes, belch without having to say excuse me, let me stay in the same hotel room with them, order myself one of those breakfasts with grapefruit cut into little pieces and some other fruit maybe cherries?

Tomorrow they'll let me know their plans but for some time now I see they're nervous, the red whip is now burgundy, as if it had been used to wipe ass.

as soon as she gets to the party
it looks like she's ready to leave

You've caught on
you know
you've guessed

if she stays in her mother's house it's to spy on her, gather the proof to send her to jail. Revenge for the death of her father.

—Don't call me Bochita anymore.

—And what am I supposed to call you? Greta? Marlene? They go well with the raincoat. It's true that divorced and all Bochita sounds too much like the girl next door, it has a certain common air about it and now you're up to something else . . .

—Juana.

—Juana? That's the name of a washerwoman, a woman who runs a *pensión* like me, for example, I could very well be called Juana, but you, on the other hand.

—Juana, like my dad. If Juan is a good enough name for him, Juana will do me very well.

—Come on. And when you could have a name like the higher-ups. Something foreign, like a perfume ad, Elizabeth, Michelle, or if you insist on a national name, Alejandra. But Juana.

—Juana.

—In any case for me you'll always be Bochita, kid.

—Juana, you fucking murderess. Juana.

—What did you say?

like a faithful dog

He was in love. Drooling. That's why they'd given him a job canning hearts of palm. He noticed nothing but followed Malvina with eyes, feet, twists of his torso but never with his hands. She passed by, flirtatious, tempting, talking about sprees, nights spent on a terrace drinking sherry by moonlight while mosquitoes had a ball biting her on the rump barely covered by scanty polka-dotted shorts.

—And then he came to me and said: Would you like me to scratch you? He was wearing gloves of the finest leather, white with some holes that let me see his pale skin because, like all the rich people of that country, he slept during the day to avoid exposing himself to the frenzy of the servants who cleaned the house, cut his toenails, and brushed his teeth with a tar previously disinfected in the urine of four virgins kept in a stable where they only drank Vichy water. I didn't see them but he'll take me to visit them, I'm sure, because they're now too old to go out alone. They're the same ones his grandfather brought back from his trip through the islands and now their kidney ailment prevents them from walking. So then, I said to him like someone who doesn't really care one way or the other: Yes, why not, but don't take off your gloves because that would be too intimate and we, well, we haven't been properly introduced.

—But, didn't he know that we all know who he is?

—Look, you're really ignorant it's not because of that, it was to show him that I have my dignity, my standards of behavior. The thing is that I believe he was accustomed to it because he scratched me all over, with the leather of the gloves grazing me with little tickles that made me laugh until I got hiccups.

—And he introduced himself to you?

—Not exactly; he said he wanted us to go more slowly, the thing about the names seemed premature to him and since he scratched me more skillfully all the time and the mosquitoes were attacking me from all sides, I swore to him that I needed

53

him with or without name and you can't imagine how much he laughed until the sun came up and the chauffeur came looking for him and I came here.

Rubén was listening and filing his nails because never in his life had he planned such a meticulous scratching. He was seeing every one of his movements, he went into the folds and creases, and while cutting hearts of palm he let them slip onto the floor and picked them up only when someone reminded him and, without seeing how, put them in cans with labels showing a smiling woman with big eyes and wearing a green hat decorated with bananas that would bring instant death to some husband who at that moment might be embracing a sweet girl at a taxi stand before going in a great hurry to a hotel. Rubén, you know by now, was in love and that's why he took every one of his manager Malvina's retellings as a gift.

He was happy with his life. His calluses softened. His belly sang at the thought of chocolates, of kisses still wet from his own semen.

This woman makes me want to jump up and down / Sing a tarantella / Shave four times an hour.

This woman
is the woman of my life.

Every morning Malvina would bring her tales of mosquitoes, sherry, beardless teenagers showing off erect pricks before her defiant eyes, dull old men who showed her rude photos taken years ago in some foreign country where they were seen in vaguely compromising positions for that time, transvestites disguised as monkeys or gorillas unable to recall their own names, a nun who discovered in her the body she would have had before playing hide-and-seek with a pervert who raped her when she was eight years old and left her turned mystic at the door of a convent when she was fifteen. Every morning
and Rubén
this is the woman of my life et cetera, et cetera

54

today they call you *perdida*,
whore, no good

Some women are loved too much and some are left worn out, stripped clean, eating meatballs with fried potatoes as if they'd never lived. They enter and leave the world without ever going on a diet or having plastic surgery, without anyone ever dreaming about them, without any fool opening his fly the better to think about them. One woman asks herself and another answers and that's all there is to it. There are those who become part of the landscape, the dead weight of a city that will never give them the time of day. She, on the other hand, is lost and they're looking for her, the girls of the cult. They neither pause nor blink. But not even she knows who she is because now she feels her name is Juana and she's very very busy.

believe me, I felt the world
was crashing down on me

Dear Diary:

Today señora Raquel caressed my cheek and when I went to give her a kiss she hit me with the red whip. It didn't really hurt or anything. Just the opposite. But she laughed, showing her teeth, and that scared me. I don't believe it was the metal and not even the beer on her breath. It was when they left me locked in and took my clothes that I realized they'd been plotting something from the beginning. It was cold. I begged them to let me out and the older one acted as if she were on my side, kicked me so the other one wouldn't catch on and while winking an eye at me said: stay calm, kid, we'll be back. The faces of the astronomers with wigs that I see on your cover when I write calmed me down, dear diary, and if I hadn't been certain I was going to come back to tell you all this I believe I would have died of the flu right then and there.

They must have taken pity on me or maybe it was a test. They came back after an hour with the uniform I'm wearing and told me doing striptease was out, smeared me with some sticky stuff and said I couldn't take off my clothes or I'd run the risk of stripping off my skin.

What a disappointment and I thought they were my friends!

sentimental education

We're going to protect you, dear, now there'll be no more shows nor any need for you to appear in public. You'll stay with us until you grow up and we can give you the role in life proper for you. They said it with conviction because I don't know what you think but I believe they had good intentions. Above all, and of this, my dear women readers and skeptical men, I have not the faintest doubt, they didn't want to make waves. It's simply that they'd discovered that discretion is a girl's greatest virtue, a girl who's just developing and whose moral sense had been eroded by the public to the point where she could no longer become

a woman with balls

an executive, carrier of a whip, mother of the poor, or fence for the rich

teacher in a reform school or head of a highly important and secret section of Interpol

Her own destiny would be stifled without these experienced protectors who, bent on killing two birds with one stone, realized that instead of continuing to search unsuccessfully for the woman of the telephone booth and the one of the Eva cult, it would be easier to invent her, uniform her, educate her.

In any case the kid's skin was of a rare type. It was as if from the beginning clothing was meant for her to take off and even later, when nude, people wanted to see more. The public believed that her very bones, veins, muscles, had some different quality, held some secret from birth, and they bought tickets, sighed, examined. She didn't know it but her armpits carried the smell of perspiration from the time on a rainy night during Carnival when her father, a boy wearing a burglar's mask, made love to a girl in a Hawaiian grass skirt beneath the awning of a marina which both had entered illegally. She carried that smell without being aware of it because nobody ever smells the fumes of their own conception but the men and women gathered to applaud her realized there were other bodies in hers and, marveling, asked for fewer and fewer articles of clothing, followed her moves with cannibalistic looks and, if two accomplices had not carried her away, someone would have raped her. Poor thing. And perhaps the worst insult after everything was over: **private autopsy.** No witnesses.

Of course at this stage of the game Raquel and Rosa hardly needed to talk to one another. They understood each other with amazing speed. To confuse people they carried cellular phones from which they made urgent calls to cafés off limits to students or anybody with subversive or slightly interesting agendas and made reservations in the names of politicians about to be arrested by the authorities. The owners instructed the waiters. That they behave very discreetly. That they bring out the most elegant pastries, that they prepare everything for a generous tip, their due reward and a bit extra and that's why when Rosa and Raquel entered they were given the best table and served like queens because they knew that recommended by this one or that one after the tea would come the big surprise, the gift that would amply justify inviting them for whatever they wanted. And they, with glances, a wink, and requests that one waiter serve them instead of another, would arrange it so that each one would think they'd given money to all the others except for them so that when they left, belching from so many delicacies, the place was in an uproar of rumors, bad feelings, and desires to testify in the trial against the politicians in whose name the reservations had been made.

It was a matter of a modest campaign against corruption.

They were a couple of show-offs

A couple of flaky fighters

One with demure panties

The other with a collection of false eyelashes inherited from the theater and kept by her bedside for years.

Using the pseudonym Fran Camufa they were now writing editorials filled with a devastating moral energy for a newspaper. They found everything bad.

The loud colors of the maids' clothes when they went out on Sundays and the funereal uniforms of the boarding school students from the nuns' school

the judges who accepted bribes from the families of juvenile delinquents to let them go free and the judges who paid innocent children to commit petty crimes that would demonstrate their human weaknesses and kept the judicial system going

mother love and the lack of children's love toward their mothers

the peace that did not allow conflicts to be resolved once and for all

the heroism of wars between combatants who didn't even speak the same language

Fran Camufa wrote editorial after editorial inciting indignation, discouragement, and the suspicion of every creature that walked. In the meantime, in the house they'd rented, the girl was growing beneath the uniform and her skin wanted to stretch but couldn't, it pulled tight beneath the gray serge and when she thought about her public a modestly thin flow trickled down between her legs. It was the closest thing to love she'd ever feel in her life. The wish to grow, take off her clothes, see their faces, lie with them at night in a cool place where they would cure all her wounds. When she managed to go to sleep she dreamed of crowds throwing kisses at her, she had the premonition of a parade of men and women dressed in harlequin suits standing in front of a balcony where she, without clothes but with a huge fan, greeted everybody without seeing a soul.

how many times must they say
what they already know?

—Don't make me repeat it again. I've said it until I'm sick of it. Twenty-four.

—OK. I'll give you one more because I like you.

—Not one more and not one less. Twenty-four.

—You must be really crazy to want twenty-four average size grapes, don't you see that anyway I sell them by the bunch? I'll have to throw them out. Do you think that perhaps I can keep them to make wine? That, only in Italy, my old man. He for sure never wasted anything; but I'm used to the good life, no jelly making for me, no using the skins of oranges to perfume the bedroom, the banana skin as a weapon, ripe bananas to make bread, rotten apples for sauce, none of that. I, if you take a look, am a thousand times more refined than you because you've got to see her with those hairy arms that look like a truck driver's and that torso, well, I don't envy it but there are people who lift weights so they'll look that way, I don't know what charm the girls see in such men but what I am sure of is that the boys wouldn't want to go with her to the movies or hold her in their arms dancing, please, don't act so high and mighty with me. I'll cut you the twenty-four but stop being such a pain in the ass with that superior air.

—How much do I owe you? I don't give a damn about your opinion or your memories of your Italian father. All that is pure show like when she shaved her mustache and told me she did it because she'd promised the girls of the cult she would pose as a virgin for their annual calendar.

—As virgin, and you, Juana, as the baby Jesus, we all need to move with the times. It can't be that we keep up this business that the baby Jesus couldn't have been Jesusa; of course if a woman dies unmarried at thirty-three years of age it's another story. If that had been the case, all of our history would have been different.

—That they crucified her for not having been able to

—or not having wanted to

—or having loved too much.

—Don't you see we're made for each other? We even agree on religion. Now that's really something.

—I want a head of lettuce that has no more than ten leaves.

—This diet is going to kill you.

—Not that it matters to you.

—Don't be like that, you fascinate me; last night I dreamed you tickled me with your beard.

—But I don't have a beard.

—Don't get mad, particularly not now that they're lining up.

—Listen to what I say. I'm on a diet and I'm not about to change it because of some stupid retail policy. When I ask for something, you give it to me, take my money period.

—Now I'm going to add up everything together, don't worry, you're not going to cheat me; the only woman who ever did was my old lady when she neglected to give me the gift of swindling the public like the politicians do.

—OK, enough chitchat, I'm in a hurry, the girls are waiting for me to continue the investigation; just give me everything like that. I'm going to leave the package there in front.

The diet was really stringent. Morning afternoon and night. A constant discipline that kept her in a state of alertness. Not a single instant without thinking about food because she had to eat every two hours. Train herself to live like a little bird. Once they'd proved what they had to prove the weight of her secret would be so great she'd have to confess that she herself had caused the death of her father in order to exonerate her mama who by that time would be old and already her rotten tricks would no longer make a dent in her but would be a sweet memory, something like it was seeing her young, energetic, and elegant, then she'd have to pay for all the crimes, her own and those of her mother and the sentence would be so long she'd have to live from crumbs, from what would be left in the cell after all the others had eaten and regurgitated. SLAVE. She would polish her bracelet and pretend indifference when she saw her name engraved. Juana the slave. She shivered with pleasure and anticipation because she had all the necessary proofs for her final abnegation, after the revenge, AFTER ALL, and would be accuser, perfect daughter, executioner; her teeth chattered, she let out a fart, she longed for a ham sandwich on bread spread with garlic butter brought especially from a German bar that was located in a very distant neighborhood, reachable only by taxi on a particularly cloudy day seated beside a guy who'd got up from the street and was looking at her with a tame and randy expression ready for whatever she might have in mind.

JUANA IN TRAINING
JUANA ALL DISCIPLINE
JUANA ALL DIETETIC CATECHISM
JUANA THE SHOW-OFF LA PINTA LA SANTA JUANITA
Lighten up!

(No need to tell me it also makes me puke but in your case I'm sure there's an element of envy.)

my hand gets sticky
just from thinking about you

Rubén went in and out of the bathroom on the sly. He didn't want anyone to see him because he was afraid they'd realize that his production was no longer up to his usual standards in canning hearts of palm. He was a man shackled by his fantasies. He saw her sliding down legs apart to fall into a tub filled with bubble bath where he was waiting wearing a suit of shiny black spandex. He saw her hiding behind a sofa at the birthday party for his grandmother panting and sweaty from all the cake and candles and he found her groping in the darkness, confused by the thin fabric of her dress and the sudden warmth of her body without underclothes. Or it was that he invited her to a movie with her mama who was in fact a cousin disguised as an older lady and the three sat, he in the middle, and there she let him kiss and touch her while the other one begged him to do the same to her. She was his kindergarten teacher and the nurse who gave him an enema the first time he got drunk. She was the boy who unthinking touched his behind as he got off the bus. He saw her wearing a tight-fitting suit but also as a nun in a Christmas choir. She was in his mother's eyes and in the walk of his older aunt. He saw her at the entrance and exit of

markets

movies

subway stations

import/export companies

the race track

the greengrocers

sometimes he saw her for real and then he felt shy, had a sudden erection that vanished the moment Malvina looked at him and said: *morning Javier, lovely day, no?*

the young are something else

SCARRED GIRL TO MAKE A STATEMENT

Crowds expected in front of the hospital

IN THE EARLY HOURS of the morning a denial was issued by the Department of Youth Services. Judge Bergorrechea refused comment to the press.

Some neighbors who prefer to remain anonymous maintain they have heard groans coming from Apartment 2-C where the young woman was found by an employee of the Don Berto stores.

Statements by the doorman and other residents of the building allowed authorities to identify two women suspects who rented the apartment and abandoned the young woman. No reasons were available.

||||||||||||||||||||||||||||||||||

BLACK CAR WITH German diplomatic plates seized in front of Parliament. International incident feared.

||||||||||||||||||||||||||||||||||

SHOCK AT TREATMENT OF SCARRED YOUNG WOMAN

Unthinkable that this would happen in a country as advanced as ours, declared the President in an exclusive interview. *"We must increase the fight against sexual abuse. This is an example that should put us all on guard,"* said Candelaria Güemes in the latest issue of the magazine *Avanzada. "Our feelings of compassion and solidarity are with the victim, we pray she finds the strength to forgive her assailants,"* stated the newspaper of the Sacred Image diocese.

The Department of Labor has promised the inspection of all households where there is domestic service with the aim of improving the situation of those who often work in conditions of real slavery. "I don't know what they were doing with the girl, at times the three seemed very happy. What a shame on top of our soccer fiasco, sometimes you feel like putting a bullet through your brain," the doorman of the building told us. (More details to come in the *Lifestyle* magazine Sunday. Don't miss it.)

—No thanks. I'm not hungry.

—But if they gave you nothing to eat. For two weeks.

—Better this way, the uniform hurts me less because my skin doesn't get pulled.

—But we're going to remove it whenever you wish.

—I don't want it removed.

—But what are you going to do? Die of starvation just to keep that rag on? Those bitches threatened you, told you they would come and find you if you took it off? Here you're among friends. Normal people. We love you. Don't be afraid of saying what's really on your mind.

—Look, I want to be left alone. I've got nothing to say. I'm not afraid.

I want to go to the bathroom. Can you tell me where it is?

—But if you go to the bathroom you're going to become dehydrated. Stay here with us. Sip a little water and later we'll let you go to the bathroom.

—No, it's not for that.

—Then what's it for?

—I need a mirror. I have to practice. It seems to me the photographers will be coming soon.

—Take it easy, that's what I say. She must have got a little crazy what with being shut up and the scars. Leave her alone. Let her do what she pleases.

—Good, go ahead: but don't think of doing anything crazy, like running away or anything like that because now you are our responsibility and if you run, my dear, we'll have to take the heat, with all due respect, we're going to watch you through the keyhole; that is if you insist on closing the door, although according to the rules it's allowed, in your case I'd like you to leave it open.

—Not open, no.

—Ajar.

—Not that either.

—Then we won't let you go.

—If you don't let me go I'll tell the reporters that it was better in the apartment even when I was starving, that I miss the señoras and that you've abused me because you like my scars. Perverts. Everybody knows it. Everybody except for me until today. That's what I'm going to tell them. So tell me where it is, you're wasting my time and I'm not going to put up with such things. Discipline. None of you have it but I have more than enough.

—Oh so the kid wants to take a pee and now she starts threatening police officers. Poor thing.

71

—Be careful, they must be recording us. Don't screw around with her because they're looking for the guilty parties and they might try to pin it on us.

—OK, that's it. Go on, dear, just go on and do your stuff, take your pee, whatever you want in total secrecy. We're only interested in your welfare, to keep you from suffering anymore and to protect the minors of this wild country that keeps on ignoring the well-being of the young to say nothing of the old.

They kept on with the blahblahblah blowing their noses, trying to get rid of the taste of tartar with mints and laughing at jokes so old they themselves had forgotten them. She, sitting in the bathroom, began her exercises. Close the eyes, practice immediately the wide-eyed look that was easier all the time because her thinness had enlarged her features. Fifteen times. And then the mouth. She was at rest and in an infinitesimal space the sweet smile with the eyes closed, concentrated on a happy moment of the times with the show. A little difficult because that part made her hungry. Meatballs she used to eat before going onstage. Cookies. A stick of gum. But here's where the question of discipline came in. Twenty times. Hands now well trained. Soon she would be ready. If they had waited a little longer. If only they'd left her a week. Fools. All those who think they understand me. Let them go to hell.
The leper girl.
Slave.
Flake.
Cutie pie.

Are you for real?

Couldn't hold it. Disgust came out his ears and gave a pasty taste to the words that came out from his lips thin lips from playing the clarinet too much spit for what he had to say. Hands scrupulously clean, nails touched up by a manicurist with bleached hair who was sweetly planning the murder of his wife so that she, lily white apron and patent leather shoes, would answer the telephone in the office: *Dr. Gutiérrez is with a patient right now. Give me your number and we'll call you the moment he's free.* In the bathroom. With dry heaves. That's how he got ready every day for the parade of patients with differing degrees of need. He looked at asses, breasts, palpated bellies, watched the advance and retreat of viruses, bacterias, obsessions that impeded breathing, boils or mere pimples on the shamed faces of teenagers who demanded an instant cure, something that would turn insults into sweet touches before the Saturday night dance doctor doctor please there must be something and he drugged himself with an impossible memory of having played the piano on a beach just before a storm that swept everything away. The sand made tears spring to his eyes and seeing how he rubbed them some alarmed patient asked if it was true that there was no hope left of recovery and assured him that a cousin in the United States would not stop in his efforts to obtain an international practice for him what a relief when Dr. Gutiérrez mentioned his allergy to city dust and prescribed some placebo to get the witnesses off his back so as to continue playing the piano beside the sea above all when the wind kicked up bringing an odor of iodine and salt, a hint of algae wrapping around his bare feet, a shiver that kept him awake, alert, something necessary when, like now, the door of the consulting room opens and the two policemen enter with Noemí:

—Here we'll leave you the Scarred Girl, Doctor. We'll expect your diagnosis shortly.

—Just examine her. Pay no attention to my companion. We

have time to spare. I even brought a pair of dice so the wait won't seem so long. That won't bother you, will it?

—Why should it bother me?

—I don't know, I ask just to be on the safe side.

—And you have conjunctivitis too? Me, I suffer from it every year at the same time just like my mother. Must be the pollution in the air.

—Thank you. You may be seated in the waiting room. The moment we're done I'll turn the patient over to you.

—Patient, what one would call a patient, no. Doesn't look to me like she's sick.

—I'll be the judge of that.

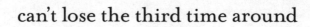
can't lose the third time around

I'll wait for you in the hospital because sooner or later you'll also fall weak sister and nothing will do you any good your changes of name and height
your diets
your buying power
I wait for you
divorcée of my dreams
this time I'll come with a box of chocolates I'll eat it in front of you tempt you the smell of chocolate jelly dripping out of the corner of my lip

surprised you'll try to make a gesture tell me I like chocolates because I remember but I won't give you the time of day I won't deprive myself of the luxury of being wanted even before you have a hint of it I know how it's going to be for you the station the train your going all that for this moment to see you and you see me without knowing I'm the nice neighbor the spy the good friend still smiling.
UNFORGIVING

MOTHER'S LOVE /
NOTHING LIKE IT

Dear Bochîta:

You'll find it odd that I write you this letter since we're living in the same house and all that but for some time now I find you very difficult. It's not that I don't like your new way of dressing. I've never had anything against women wearing suits and ties, I even think it gives a very distinguished air, something like Marlene Dietrich or Katherine Hepburn and I'm also not bothered by your diet and your facial hair or that you call yourself Juana but why refuse to speak to the boarders? Why call me the accused? Bochîta, I do not agree with what they say to me here but I beg you to see a shrink. That will make us all feel better.

Affectionately, your mama

MME. MARÍA DEL CARPIO:

I request that you present yourself in my room tonight at 8:30 for the purpose of responding to certain questions regarding the death of your husband, my father. You may bring all pertinent documents to support your credibility.

Juana del Carpio

Dear Bochîta:

Please. Instead of meeting in your room I ask you to act like a normal girl and come have supper with us in the dining room. The boarders have been gossiping about your mental state and I suspect they're afraid you might do something to endanger them. Come to eat and later we'll talk as much as you like. I'm cooking a hearts of palm quiche especially for you since you know how much your dad, may he rest in peace, liked it. The last week of his life he asked me to serve it to him for dinner every night.

Until tonight, my dear.
mama

he speaks from the groin I smell his legs the hair I don't need to touch him to prove it because I hear his voice on the telephone and can't resist it it's as though I never went away that's why when he asked for Matilde Felipa I didn't want to answer him although I'm already smaller and it will do no good to tell him I killed him and am atoning for the crime under this name and all the others it will do no good because I'm behind on line once again and I can't help it I see myself open-mouthed quivering swept away by that fury his voice comes to me and here I am groping for a fly zipper dark corners hallways he's a fake like the other ones wants to make me disappear swallow me baptize me and then I'll be his voice his touch on my head as I kneel down.

III

who does he think he is?

—Does it hurt when I touch you?

—I'm used to it but you don't need to use force, the glue they put on me is forceps proof.

—Did you know they were going to do this to you? How did they manage to spread it so evenly? With a move this way and that you could have prevented the uniform from clinging so tightly to your body, it would have left us a chink so we could have taken it off you.

—All in all I don't care if nobody's interested in what I've got underneath now.

—You're pretending to be crazy so we'll put you in one of those clinics where they'll give you nice pills that will cheer you up or make you sleep or go like a sleepwalker singing children's songs. But you're very mistaken because I'm not one of those, that's why they brought you here. They know I won't give up on you until I'm sure we can get to the bottom of your case, or know there's no hope left.

—Look at me, look at me all you want, you won't be able to prove anything.

—Stay right there. I'm going to turn on the water heater in the bathroom, we'll immerse you in steam and you'll see how the uniform will come loose. You'll be like new. They all come here just for that. I give them a peeling, they come out with raw skin but it's worthwhile because when their husbands touch them they tremble and that's a miraculous cure for couples dried up by routine. I don't know why they insist on and on with the same thing. Twenty. Thirty years. What else could they do? Since there's no divorce, peeling. And the drama of forbidden pleasures returns. No not there it hurts me then the guys get more excited and the women begin to like it; after a while most of them tell me they love it. You have no idea how many come back over and over. This business of the uniform and the glue is not bad, it would save me a bundle in moisturizers, masks, creams, and all that.

—You're the one who's crazy. That sort of thing does nothing for me. I don't have a husband. If I shiver it's because I need fresh air. I go days, months perhaps without seeing the light of day or breathing fresh air. I want to breathe.

—They didn't let you go out? They kept you prisoner?

—Prisoner as such, no. But between the show first and the señoras later, I didn't breathe and I see I really want to. Haven't you ever thought of how beautiful it would be to go to the beach? You must have a car, all doctors have cars. Let's go to a deserted beach where we'll be the only ones to breathe the air. A beach with no tourists, no kids, no tents, no vendors, and no carbonated drinks. A plain old beach. That's where I want to go.

—I might fall in love with you.

—Oh, no doubt. Everybody falls in love with me. That's why I want to breathe a little before having to get into that stuff.

—OK, I'll have the guards come in and I'm going to tell them I'd like to hold you for observation in my clinic until three o'clock tomorrow afternoon.

—Look, Doctor, excuse the interruption but we just heard the entire conversation you had with this freak.

—But how can you allow yourselves such insolence . . . spying on a doctor.

—Come on, don't make yourself out to be so pure, you're like everybody else and you know how things work in this country. Here we eat from what we can hear and we fill our wallets with what they ask us to forget. Go wherever you please. But this is a very awkward situation and will require a hefty contribution for my colleague and myself, enough that will allow us, well, to have lost the Scarred Girl in the traffic or in the woods or in unexplained circumstances.

—Let's say she went crazy and threw herself in the river. Or that her family finally turned up and registered her in a Swiss school where they'll teach her languages, how to eat lobster, to ski sporting a white parka with a fur hood. How we'll enjoy the photographs she'll send until, horrified, scrutinizing attentively, we discover she's still wearing the uniform. Poor Scarred Girl, bent beneath her spandex suit.

—I like the way these men talk. The moment will come when I can thank them for what they've done for me. For now, I want to leave you a gold garter the señora gave me. Don't sell it. It's just for you to show me when I come back.

BECAUSE I'LL COME BACK
I'LL COME LOOKING FOR YOU
DEAR GUARDS
MY DEAR PROTECTORS
SCARRED NO MORE
UNIFORMED NO MORE
    I'LL COME BACK IN SKI CLOTHES
    I'LL COME BACK IN A TUTU
    AND AN ERMINE WRAP
I'll come back to eat polenta, make a barbeque.

—Look how she makes tears come to my eyes.

—No, don't give us anything, Doctor. Take her away, she's suffered more than enough. Make her happy. We'll take charge of the clinic. Nobody will notice anything after all. Not even medicines remain in the pharmacies. Let her live her life. Poor Scarred Girl.

—Do you want to touch me?

—Touch what?

—The scar of my heart . . .

—I don't dare, it gives me the creeps.

—I will, it'll bring me good luck.

—Just a moment. It's twenty pesos.

who cares?

They kiss each other on moonlit nights. They're lying in a hammock and he no longer needs tamed mosquitoes to scratch her buttocks nor does she wear any more provocative shorts. Now she goes naked with tattoos that simulate a formal tweed suit with black buttons and a secretary's skirt. But he knows that she like all the other women on the island has taken her clothes off for him and then he caresses her as if he were mashing beans, molds her and eats her when she's ready while she whimpers something that he believes is her name because they still haven't been introduced. He doesn't want to compromise himself. A man in his position is preparing for something different. A man in his position requires anonymity for his love affairs but she pretends not to know and lying in the hammock acts as if she were dressed and says: don't wrinkle my collar or you just ruined the pleat of my jacket and he enchanted by her voice and her cautions does not protest, says it's all right now, only a bit more but he lingers and keeps going because now he knows that behind him is Rubén, the melancholy guy that takes in everything thinking himself invisible. One of these days, says Rubén to himself, I'll invite them to eat hearts of palm but the other keeps on and now, raised over her looking straight at Rubén has a splashy orgasm.

beautiful *muñequita* /
dear little Goldilocks

WHERE IS THE SCARRED GIRL?
POLICE SEARCH CONTINUES

||||||||||||||||||||||||||||||||

—Look, I always wanted a girl. Boys are so boring. Girls, everybody knows, are a mother's soul mate. They go shopping with her, tell her little secrets, ask advice, imitate her way of dressing.

—To feel admired by a girl exactly when men start to lose interest.

—And people say *they look like sisters.*

—But after all they're women just like all the others.

ENVIOUS

GOSSIPY

SELF-CENTERED

—There you go again with all that; look sometimes you make me think of a brother of mine, but obviously he likes guys. He doesn't realize it but he likes guys.

—He doesn't realize it?

—No. He's always watched them as they walked along the street, criticized the girls to them, went to soccer games, told them everything he did with his sweetheart, drank beer, made everybody's life miserable except for my mother who thought he was a saint and to this day doesn't understand that if he cheated on his wife it was not her fault, poor thing, so hard-working although, clearly, with all those humiliations she's let herself go to some extent and makes it even seem she might deserve what she gets.

—Let yourself go, that's a no-no.

—But with things so expensive, just buying lipstick is a big deal.

—But see there's no need for a lot of makeup. I think a balanced diet and clean clothes are enough, above all at our age when there are some who even start to smell bad.

—I thank God I found this *pensión*. We've got everything we need. It's not cheap but you are an exceptional landlady.

—Tell that to my Bochita. I don't know what's got into her with the business of calling me the accused. Writing me letters and all that. I had no other recourse than to tell her I would appear tonight.

—And you're going alone? I think it's best that we boarders be present, I say it just in case.

—Why? Don't tell me you think the kid is going to harm me, attack me. There are so many women who change their names, so many who go on diets and about the facial hair, well, it's a hormonal problem that the poor thing can't control. As for me personally, I'm glad she's acquired some individuality, that she's assertive and I even believe the greengrocer is getting fond of her. The dream of my life is that she marries someone from the neighborhood, has children, takes them to play in the square. Then for sure I'd sell the *pensión*. My grandchildren are going to be as beautiful as she was when she was a little girl. A doll.

nuestro amor / más que amor / es un castigo
love you no matter what, baby

Pascual Domenico managed to get up from the floor by himself where she had left him for dead after taking a shot at him. He called a taxi and went to the nearest hospital and swore to them he'd wounded himself while cleaning his gun. In a couple of days he was as good as new and began the search that now, after two years, three months, four days, and a minute, culminated in this call.

—I don't care if you're unrecognizable.

—I have a trial pending

—but my love, you're not a lawyer.

—it's not that, I'm the prosecutor and today I have to present the charges.

—I've searched for you so long I cannot wait, I cannot accept your telling me we can't see each other now that I've found you.

—I've changed; I'm a different person.

—A treasure like you doesn't change but only gets better

—I have another name

—the name is a minor matter, I'm not even going to ask you, *cosita de papá,* baby girl

—but I tell you you're going to be disappointed

—to pick you up in my arms again, carry you to the bedroom; I made you a little stool carved with our names so you can climb up when you have to get a can of tomatoes from the cupboard to make me that tomato sauce, the special marinara that drove me crazy

—marinara on Sundays

It was a depilatory conversation. Juana's facial hair began to fall out and if she hadn't had the presence of mind to shorten the slacks in time she would have ended up stumbling on the cuffs now too long to allow her to walk quickly. But she cheered up and taking out a small bit of lettuce stuck it between her teeth and went out noisily to the street to breathe, find herself once again in the wind and the rain. Pascual Domenico sang a ballad to her in her innards; made her want to eat ricotta cheese, gnocchi, steak. Pascual Domenico's voice said her hair was uncombed, that she should catch a cold so he could take care of her and when she was strong once more and they loved each other anew with an unquestionable and serene love, she would be free to find the pistol again, come into the room, shoot him, steal the key to the door, and leave him on the floor to bleed to death.

Dizzy with that cottony and circular future, she held up her slacks with uneven hands, not caring now that people saw her in the act of shrinking or that the greengrocer stopped giving her the best lettuce from the cart. As happened often, the girls of the Eva cult passed by her with no sign of recognition. They went singing in blustery fashion, pretending to be crazy, because this week it happened that every one of them was suffering from premenstrual tension and according to a medical prescription had to chant special hymns for the occasion. A gang of boys followed them with signs, bells, and invitations to dances in dark houses where the father of one of them, a short paunchy gentleman, counted ticket after ticket seated at a marble table with a glass of chocolate milk at his left hand.

siamese twins!

At night when he went to bed he couldn't close the door because he had the illusion that she was going to decide to leave and wasn't going to find the key. He was fed up with the decorations she'd brought to the room. Fed up with her scenes of domesticity and eyes rolled back when speaking of her saintly mother. When they lived in separate rooms they spied on each other, reinterpreting every little noise as a signal, sensing their dreams and while washing their faces in the morning felt curious about the temperature of the other's cheeks, the intuition of their movements and an unconditional passion for everything concerning their drowsiness, their letting go onto the pillow.

They lived with colds because of the drafts, particularly in winter, but she also expects something from the open door and didn't dare say *it's cold I want to be nice and warm inside*. Rubén and Marta are pensive and calculating lovers. They're always on the alert, ready for any possibility that arises. He, we now know, is in love with the foolish voluble Malvina. She will keep revealing her life to us little by little because that's her style, don't give everything away at once. She works as a secretary in a circus that came from India and kept deciding to stay one more day until all the passports and permits for transporting animals expired. The seventy-five illegal immigrants that made up the circus are her bosses. That's why she's so satisfied with her work. She doesn't make much but extorts whatever money she wants from them whenever she likes. She's ambitious. A woman ready to step on the gas and snatch away candy from her bosses' mouths just when they think they're safe. If that is not power, tell me, you smart and arrogant readers of novels, what is.

Let's catch up on the news

Dear Diary:

   Finally a moment to talk to you. Dr. Gutiérrez is very different from the señoras. He wants nothing from me. It's as if he'd forgotten that we came here together. He spends the entire day walking along the seashore even when it's raining. We've not been seven days in this cabin. He doesn't talk to me but takes me with him and hasn't left me alone one moment until today. I think he's afraid I might escape. If he only knew that I have no place to go. Last night he put one of his sweaters on my bed and asked me to wear it over the uniform so as not to catch cold. Poor thing, he doesn't realize that nothing of that sort affects me. But all the same I thanked him and today I'm going to put on the sweater and try to talk to him because I believe he's a very well mannered doctor although it makes me feel odd when he starts playing with his toes after brushing off the sand picked up from the beach. It's logical that I cannot bathe myself. To me it seems that he, as a man of science, should do it. At least that's what they taught us in school.

How IS ONE TO REACT faced with a group of corrupt officials who lie about everything? Today Lt. Fontana flatly denied being involved in the disappearance of the minor sadly known as the Scarred Girl. Commissioner Rekiewicz corroborated his statements with documentation that showed that Lt. Fontana and his partner were in headquarters working on the file of orphans that by law must be brought up to date before the end of the current year. Nevertheless, the testimony of a dozen eyewitnesses leaves no room for doubt: the girl disappeared while under their protection in the doctor's clinic.

In the present materialistic and antipatriotic atmosphere the worst conjectures come to mind: has she been sold to a foreign circus in order to be exhibited? Has she been kidnapped by a guerrilla group to be used as hostage in their antipatriotic cause?

We demand a reply. Every citizen, male, female, and child, should answer the call. Let us show our indignation in face of the official silence tomorrow morning at eleven o'clock at the Governmental Palace.

Fran Camufa
(*La Provincia Daily*)

||||||||||||||||||||||||||||||||

IT IS INDEED ABSURD that at this moment of serious hardships and changes in the economic policy of our country so much expense should be incurred in finding the so-called Scarred Girl. Why should one take so much interest in a sleazy local story? How many orphans in our country have been abandoned to strangers by irresponsible parents? Clearly the interest expressed by governmental sources is a way of creating a smoke screen that keeps us from realizing the errors that have occurred in the leadership of the country.

Let us say no to confusion and sensationalism. Let us dedicate ourselves to the true tasks of citizenship. We all know that we women find true satisfaction at home, in the tranquility of our occupations and in the transformation of the society through the democratic exercise of the vote. Citizens: let us return to our houses. Let us not join demonstrations or be drawn into the games of diversionist forces. Such is our duty. Our strength lies in doing nothing.

Fran Camufa
(*Capitalina Daily Journal*)

||||||||||||||||||||||||||||||||

Letters from Readers to the *Magazine of Science, Society, and Style*

RECENT EVENTS SURROUNDING the disappearance of Miss Noemí point up the necessity of completely abolishing the use of uniforms for civilian work. We express our condemnation of the acts of aggression against her person and urge a boycott of the multinationals whose products endanger our most beloved traditions.

Lic. Francisco L. Mendieta
General Manager
National Society of Clothing Manufacturers

Rosa María Montander
President
National Organization of Business Employees

||||||||||||||||||||||||||||||||

IN THE FIRST PLACE one has to ask what that girl was doing in an apartment with two mature women who were not her blood relatives. Let us not be confused about the true martyrs of our country: the women who live as

God commands, keeping the peace and harmony of the family in contrast to a woman with no morals who despite her youth is an example of all the spiritual failures of our society.

Dr. Alberto Bignotazzi
Specialist in Diseases of the Skin and Scalp

||||||||||||||||||||||||||||||||||

I WISH TO USE your pages to send a message of love to the Scarred Girl. I also suffer from leprosy and live hidden beneath my clothes. One day we shall meet and be happy.

||||||||||||||||||||||||||||||||||

THE UNDERSIGNED wish to assure Miss Noemí that she can return to her country and leave her kidnappers who are most certainly spoiling her with promises of a better life in a foreign country with barbaric customs. Together we will make her scars disappear in the seaside complex we have named in her honor and where there will always be a cottage reserved for her.

(one hundred and fifty signatories)
Association of Hotel Keepers
"La Llagadita"
The Scarred Girl Seaside Complex

||||||||||||||||||||||||||||||||||

WARNING TO THE PUBLIC
The young woman, Noemí Gaviria, alias the Leper Girl, alias the Scarred Girl, may be infected with a highly contagious disease not yet diagnosed. Immediate notification to the Police is requested if her whereabouts are known. All physical contact with her should be avoided as well as any action that involves breathing the same air.

PROTECT YOUR HEALTH
HONOR YOUR COUNTRY

Clean in the morning
and two hours later it's dusty again

Marta is typing away. The circus is in a state of crisis. The animals are old and pestered by kids who throw peanuts to them and take photos putting on a ferocious face like people going off on a safari. The illegal workers have fallen in love, cheated, and hooked up with one or another so many times they've forgotten which one was their first love and have ended up living all together an amoebalike existence. Marta's blackmail schemes don't matter to them. They give her everything and even enjoy doing so because it lets them call her **her excellency the loan shark** when they can do no more and go to ask her to let them see that photo of her mama or of the aunt or the first lion cub born in captivity that she'd shown them one day on a pure whim or clippers because with the cold the elephants' skin had dried out and every time they had to clean them they broke their nails. She types types types the offenses, the debts, the arrears, sweats and the drops of sweat dry on her forehead so as not to ruin the list or lose the inventory she'll have to buy a computer modernize above all now there are children and the seventy-five original illegals have doubled and soon their number will grow even higher. They're like rabbits since they no longer talk about love. They reproduce just because, to find a mirror, this shit of this country, nurse with a milk without nostalgia of those moonlit nights when they consulted a fortune-teller who said they should not leave for a remote country where they speak a brutal language with open vowels and consonants that are pronounced the way they're written, what an insult. Selfless, Rubén calls her because she hasn't told him she has a secret deposit with every object properly labeled. He doesn't know that the illegals have been working for some time on her recommendations in obscure plants loading and unloading very heavy packages that levitate thanks to their contents of miraculous mushrooms that change the mood of adolescents who trade their lives in exchange for a speedy trip to a place with artificial fireworks and colored feathers. We'd like to think that if he knew it, he'd be outraged but the truth is Malvina has seduced him completely with her hips, her strong smell of female in heat and he had no time to think of anything except the arrangements necessary to change his name, to be Javier. What lack of sensitivity to say to her: I'm Rubén miss because he didn't want her to know he remembered that she is Malvina. Better Javier. Better to arrange the papers formally so that when they get married she won't feel bad. In the meantime, Marta amasses a powerful fortune and soon will have to make her own plans because the illegals don't like to work for a woman who looks poor and goes about on foot. She'll have to get a car, make them see that her power rests on money, hand them a few tips, give them something for the many babies, perhaps run for the presidency or a governorship. After all there's danger that the immigration law might be changed and if they give visas to these interlopers everything will come to a standstill.

Rubén waited for her with open arms. Today he's seen Malvina's heels up close. He'd dropped a heart of palm just as she passed by and had to pick it up quickly so she wouldn't stumble. He even smelled her tanning lotion mixed with insect repellent and realized that on this particular night she wouldn't be with that son of a bitch suitor.

No scratching. It was crucial that he perfect his erotic skills because once Malvina could do without the other's embraces it would be a question of aiding chance and making her his own. Marta comes into the room a little tired with her head full of numbers and symbols of ghost countries through which she laundered the money from the levitating packages. When he kisses her she feels a new urgency, something that cut through her distraction and calculations. Out of courtesy before undressing him she says *I love you so much* and doesn't hear when he says not me because when he nibbles her ear she leaves noisily for the movies where her first sweetheart had taught her all those things the years helped her to forget.

The workers in the hearts of palm factory had begun to read the news from abroad thanks to the e-mail of the company's computer. They send a delegate who gives them soccer scores, the vicissitudes concerning the visits of the pope, and, most of all, the scandals caused by the girls of the Eva cult who go about biting every apple they run across because they regard the sale of apples a sacrilege if done without prior mention of her, the Sought Woman, the admired, the lady with the reversible coat.

The people adore the girls, those who wear orthodontic braces and also those with perfect or rotten teeth, those with big bottoms and with flat asses. They want to do something. A collection. But they know these girls do not accept money, only clues and contests of fortune-telling that allow them to advance their cause. Noemí's story does not move them. Fool. It's all her fault. Leave her in uniform. Here they're not in agreement. Twenty thousand deaths a year. Twenty-one thousand in three months and that's how the number of botulism cases is growing. It's the hearts of palm. It's the hearts of palm from that canning factory. The autopsies say so. Interrupted conversations. Shock. Obviously they were very careless, obviously, but they worked according to orders from above. And now they're going to have to tell it all. The e-mail announced it and it would be in the newspapers when the police interrogate all of them. One by one. Idiots. Absentminded. Lovesick. Head in the clouds. Murderers.

That Juana who made the accusation must be nuts. Paranoid. Certainly they'd find plenty of psychiatrists to testify that all of this has been a terrible mistake caused by the moonlit lights, the mosquitoes, the slimy servitude of every sensitive heart.

maybe you'll simply call yourself maría

—No. There's no Matilde Felipa here. Don't insist.

—This photo doesn't ring a bell with you? Or this other one? We're posing in front of a telephone booth. Of course to you it might look like just anything, you may not even have noticed it's a booth; people forget details but for us it was a very important place. Look, sometimes when I look at her and think of her being who knows where, lost in the crowd because she's so short, you understand. In this shot it's clear as day. She barely came up to my shoulder and when she became kittenish it seemed she shrank.

—It's obvious you love her very much, but what do you want me to do. She's not here. Although the face has something I can't quite grasp. It seems familiar to me. Let me look more closely. Flowers inside the booth? Amazing about optical illusions. I would've sworn they were flowers. Tulips. It must be the reflection of the pattern of some dress, who knows. She looks sweet, Matilde, except for the height and that very delicate skin I would say she resembles my daughter Bochita. She was such a sweet girl and now she's turned into a wild beast, what life does to you and you with Matilde who left you and doesn't write or anything.

—But I know she's here. I talked to her on the phone and everything. I demand that you give me a list of your boarders.

—No, no. That's private. Nobody wants to hide anything, you understand, but this is a reputable *pensión*. Nobody wants someone to come sniffing about in their lives, above all in this country where once they find you they invent some motive, accuse you of a robbery here, smuggling there and finally with the mania about the Scarred Girl, crimes against minors and endangering the public health. Forget it. I will not give you the list.

—This will make you change your mind. It's the same pistol with which Matildita meant to split my heart but I guarantee you I'm a good shot and I'll do you in.

—She shot you? And you're looking for her. Now that's what they call love. Would that my dear departed could have viewed life with that sort of romanticism. Instead, on and on about the food, this quiche and that stew and that other dish his obsession with the hearts of palm for which I thank heavens but that's another story. Look, stop pointing that gun at me. I'm only a poor old lady and this way I'll die of a heart attack before you find the cutie and we can celebrate. I will not give you the list but I could invite you to eat supper with us tonight and take part in the trial later.

—A trial? Are you sure that all the boarders will come?

—Absolutely sure. Nobody misses mealtimes and in addition, they're curious to see what happens.

They talked, compared the length of their hair, wept. Each one caught up in his or her own situation. Each one hoping that the other would erect a monument to their exemplary suffering. Because they loved each other. She with a mother's love learned from the movies, television, and from spying on a woman next door who received a visit every afternoon from her spinster niece for tea. That should have been her life. The more she thought of it the more tears she shed. Companionship. The true companionship of an unmarried daughter who would have tea with her mama always at the same hour except when the mama, attractive, glamorous in a satin gown, has not been able to extricate herself from the arms of her lover with black mustache and incredibly long fingers one with a ring he's stolen from the head of a drug cartel, then the daughter waits alone and pensive because for her there's nothing better in life than mother's love and since she's known it forever she doesn't look elsewhere, doesn't travel, never makes a mistake, never does anything to embarrass anyone. A wallflower she's a girl who always remembers the birthdays of her mama and her girlfriends with gifts she makes herself. She's been so well raised everybody says: she's so perfect it brings tears to your eyes. Pascual Domenico was also weeping for very obvious reasons, a love that kills. Womanizer, wearing a pin-striped suit, we'd feel more sympathy for him if his breath didn't smell the way it does.

te llamabas rosicler / como el primer rayo del día
and I've got you under my skin
my own sweet climbing rose

—Turn off the radio. That melody makes me sad. It's like what people in our neighborhood used to listen to when I was a little girl.

—And you don't like to think about when you were a little girl? I'm older than you and that's why I get things somewhat mixed up but that's the only thing I truly enjoy. To recall or pretend something could have happened. For example now that we're on the beach I feel I'm a five-year-old kid playing with a girlfriend and that's why I don't want it to be in secret, I don't want to run the risk that you'll leave and I'll be left alone and bored but when you look at me as you're doing right now I get disappointed because you don't have the expression of a little girl but of a woman who's been around too long, too much wear and tear in your face, my dear.

—I didn't come here to play hide-and-seek. I wanted to escape for a while to be able to keep doing the exercises the señoras recommended to me, Rosa and Raquel. I've reached a certain level of expertise but I'm afraid so much chatting is making me lose the skill and then yes I'll stay trapped in a uniform forever.

—I was sure of it. You don't like that uniform either. Let me rid you of it. I even promise I'll do it without hurting you.

—You don't understand anything. The business I'm involved in has nothing to do with what's taught in universities, the experiments with corpses or whatever, those things in formaldehyde that must have been the thing back when you were a medical student because you've got a few years on you, I'm not saying you're old, see? Don't misunderstand me when I say I like to watch you when we go out for a walk along the beach and your mouth and your nose seem to change shape and at times I even believe that I can feel the quality of the air you're breathing because for me there's not much difference, you know. I find this beach kind of disappointing. I thought it would be different.

109

—You're a strange kid. At our age nobody wants a change of air. This beach has everything I need but if you don't like it we'll go somewhere else. I'll call the pharmacist and ask him to alternate the medicines among my patients, at bottom they're all done for. I've been doing the same thing for years. They're so used to rejoicing for having one more day they take my absence as a vacation. Let's go. I want to get you out of here, but let me help you with the uniform.

—I don't need help. Maybe only to call the señoras to let them know I'm all right.

—Those creeps. Go, call them and then finally people will know where they are and give them what they've got coming. It's a good idea. They can't blame you for having blown their cover.

—You treat me as if I were stupid. The only help I need is a phone so I can talk to them and leave them a message at a location I know.

—Aren't you going to tell me anything? After all that's happened you should have already realized that I'm going to throw everything overboard for your sake. I'll do whatever you want. I'll keep our secrets and if you wish I'll hide myself in some uniform or other and we'll go out and parade around together and who knows people may even throw confetti at us.

—Look I can also make jokes.

—It's not a joke. I left all those walking dead in my waiting room, I left my family, but what's the use? Why bore you with it. A young girl in a uniform like you has never bothered to think of such things. You're doing the right thing, I suppose.

—As for thinking, I do think. Thanks for the money. If you have to come with me to the phone booth, turn your back while I'm dialing because I don't want you to see the number.

—Hi. Yes it's me. Well, everything's fine. A little earlier than we thought.

—Sure. Tomorrow.

—Tonight?

—Why not? Although I'm a bit nervous.

—Now I feel better. So long.

—Me too.

—I'm not asking you to tell me what they did to you or why you're attached to them but we're leaving this very day whether you want to or not. We're leaving here and going to a place where we won't have to hide or say anything to anybody about the uniform. I'm sick and tired of this running around, the calls for public pity, that's why I stayed there, getting bloated in my office collecting funds for orphan asylums that certainly need it. No, my dear, from now on, a new life. But what are you doing? Wasn't it the case that you never needed to go to the bathroom? Go ahead, go by yourself since I no longer care if you run away. What's it to me? But come back and give me a good-bye kiss.

After ten minutes, dear friends, she came out of the bathroom. Ready to travel. Blue leather overnight case in her hand and under her arm, carefully folded, the uniform a bit darker than he remembered because she was diligent and had washed all the spots. If only so that when they put it in a museum they wouldn't say she'd been filthy.

follow you wherever you go

that woman is running along a street that leads to five corners   reflected in her eyes the lights of a café where a man is
waiting for her   she can see him in the distance knows his
breath feels the weight of his arm on her shoulder   manages
to feel sheltered by his proximity he always sits eyes fixed on
the window   at times he's distracted   as he puts a sugar cube
in his coffee cold by now   because he's been there for hours
a waiter comes and smiles at him but he pays no attention because he's elsewhere *he's really waiting for me* she tells herself
and then tries to run faster but the street is made of synthetic
foam and now a rain of huge black cottony drops starts to fall

my heart is running wild

—I don't have time to talk about such things. Pay me the rent next week. Wait, help me with the zipper of this sweater. The last time I wore it was for her sweet-sixteen party. And now look, look at me.

—Myself I think you're exaggerating, your daughter is strange but she's not going to subject you to a real trial, it's only to scare you.

—Court-martial she said the last time. *What a pity there's no court-martial for people like you.*

—It's all these military governments that have gone to the heads of young people. Imagine, growing up like they did. Their brains must be full of marches and communiqués to the population.

—Don't give me that, Bochita was a little girl when she got married and left here and if she hadn't got divorced from that saint she could even have given me grandchildren and everything. No, she never had the slightest interest in politics. Just the other way around, she made fun of the deceased who always had opinions about everything.

—This tailored suit looks good on you. Why not wear Bochita's hat? Now that she's shorter she certainly won't wish to wear a hat anymore, it would make her look like a mushroom, so squatty. A shame, I admit I liked Marlene.

—lately with the facial hair and the hat she reminded me of Rivero.

—oh him yes he sang very well; to me Gardel always seemed a bit effeminate. I like tango with a macho voice.

—We're from another time, not like Bochita who's from none.

She arrived. Red-faced. Out of breath, with a file of papers from the hearts of palm cannery. Her slacks now resembled an accordion, her blouse had disappeared and her breasts in the air had drops of sweat that gleamed when the light fell on them a certain way. *Big tits* she heard Domínguez the professor of history say. *Mamita* the greengrocer whispered in her ear as he passed by to take his place in the jury box. *Bring out the defendant,* she ordered. But her mother now entered alone, disheveled and pale with the hat tilted to one side and the look of a traveler about to disembark in an excessively humid country.

—Take off those stockings. Here no imposters are allowed. Also the high heels and that ridiculous suit.

—Just like that, in front of everybody? That's a lack of respect, come on Bochita, have a little sense.

—If you don't do it I'll shoot myself right now.

Great shock in the room at the sight of the pistol. She showed her teeth, she had a brilliant happy smile and when she pointed the gun at her head she could see that the nurse of Room 3 had fainted in the arms of her niece and that the two boys who looked like twins clasped hands while a dark spot spread on the pants of the skinny one who would stare during the entire trial shamefaced at the puddle that had formed in front of his patent leather shoes.

you took the best   why not the rest?

Wearing feathers, in gala costume, she spun around and around like a top in front of the pregnant women cyclists. They talked to her in loud voices, shouted at her. Clicking castanets and her red heels, she wiggled her waist and winked at them. She was totally captivated by her own charms and had no time to waste. She'd organized competitions of

grass skating

mountain climbing on shredded paper

recital of poems in twenty languages simultaneously by choruses of boys with cracking voices

diaper changing

coitus in the third age of life

Latin tongue twisters

washing and ironing of sheets

race walking on hands

poker canasta *truco* chess blackjack monte russian roulette

and later had passed out smiles diplomas thrown kisses written letters that's why she still shows a power of concentration that's left them stunned because now she's spent several days in that incessant dance and they'd had to rotate the pregnant cyclists because those ready to give birth leave for places where there are no houses or apartments only pastures and some cows so that the children would grow up without knowing about masturbatory siestas in cities with men and women who caressing a knee will inculcate in them the desire to meet another child in the square   twenty years later that child will take them by the hand to a dank and cavernous prison from which they will not come out until it's too late   such good mothers those cyclists nothing like them.

They can all be rotated except for her. Spinning she whirls, pauses an instant, gives them the whip of her perfect eyelashes and when everybody has gone she keeps going for herself alone. Magnificent iron doll. No longer a poor little girl. Not a trace of the scars.

They're alone and Dr. Gutiérrez at her feet exhausted by love dreams of her day and night canonizes her and beats the hell out of her. But the minute he awakes he sees her, erect, grave, unable to tell him that secret that he wishes to wheedle from her day and night. In any case, he hardly sleeps, his ear always ready to catch her words, he dedicates songs to her, wants to ingratiate himself so she'll let him polish her skin with antirust solutions. She rejects the idea:

she likes the fact that her body darkens with use, senses there's another one underneath and that it wouldn't be difficult to assemble it. And they thought she was a scarred girl

a leper girl

a flea

I believe she's always loved us and when she dances she offers us a charm that makes us young again   a lottery ticket   an armoire full of magnificent clothes   wraps with sequins and love letters written by swains of the silent movies. I'd follow her too even though I'm walking behind the other, cheat, untrustworthy girlfriend.

Do you need a visa to go there?

—I don't have the locket. I don't know what you're talking about.

—But oh honorable Loan Shark. I need it to prove my birth, I don't have any other document and I want to get a passport.

—Passports aren't necessary if you wish to remain in the country. Ungrateful thing. With all the food we've given you, with all the circus tickets children and old people have bought to see you and this in a country that, as you know, lacks everything. Go away, where? Pack your bags and put what in them? What if you've given everything to me knowing you wouldn't be able to get it back? Outside the distances are different. Don't be fooled. Not one of those who arrive thinking they're going to leave ever does. Think about it. It's far away. Don't pretend to be tourists, you'd be recognized wherever you go. You look like hoboes. Smelling of cigarettes and clothes put together at random. Everywhere people will say:

This one's not going into the souvenir shops

this one doesn't ask where he can find the best typical dishes nor will he bargain over the price of some piece of junk only to fish out a wad of showy dollars and pay with one wrinkled bill he carries hidden in his right sock because it brings him good luck

I won't have my picture taken with this one or exchange addresses with him.

He's my twin brother and it's useless for him to try something he knows nothing about we've got you figured out got our eyes on you we know you very very well don't give yourself airs or keep looking for an escape hatch

When she finished singing she was out of breath, then he unbuttoned her blouse and began to caress her patiently because he didn't want to rush things, he smeared jelly over her, licked her until he'd had enough of it and thought twice before proposing to her that they leave together that very afternoon in a boat he'd been preparing for months for his wife and three children not realizing that from the beginning it was meant for the loan shark and her eternal debtor. Through his breath and his saliva she'd entered a hut where a dark-haired woman, perhaps his mother or an aunt, looked at him harshly before slapping him across the face. In a corner a chubby man whom he'd called father was sewing something white, probably a bridal gown. When he heard the sound of the slap the tailor began to whisper something in a language she couldn't understand and he, bleeding, knelt before the woman obediently and ate some thick brown soup from the floor.

    —No, look, I don't think it's a good idea for us to go away together.

    —That's a relief. I asked for politeness' sake. After a feast like this.

    —Now I have to take a shower.

    —No, it's not necessary. I'll take care of it.

And they started in again but now the tailor had disappeared and she didn't care about the soup because she'd discovered the purpose of her job as secretary, the point of being a loan shark and with a tourist's enthusiasm abandoned herself to the caresses of her debtor, now neither respectful nor timid offering her incomprehensible words in a daring, insolent, somewhat sadistic voice.

(mine met each other
while doing a fox-trot)

Analía offered her hand to Pascual Domenico Fracci because when she saw him crossing the street with his eyes half
closed she thought he was blind not realizing he was thinking
about Juana. He took her hand immediately not caring that
just then she was dressed as a nun although at another time he
would have rejected her given the fuss the parish church made
when he left his wife and children.

—Where may I take you, sir?

—Would you like a cup of coffee, sister?

—Ah, you say that because of the disguise. I'm not a nun,
I'm here because of the ad.

—Is it difficult to enter the group? They must be like a political party those girls.

—No, you're mistaken. They are really motivated. They want
to find the chief of the Eva cult, recuperate the taste of the apples, that's all. Look, it doesn't seem to interest you. Something
about greengrocers, I said to myself, but out of curiosity I
turned up at the meeting and liked it very much. They're so serious. So charming. I'm not used to women who look me
straight in the eye. Or who interview me or offer me a salary.
Your disguise seems very good to me, one curly haired one said
to me. No, the señora was not religious, a nun would frighten
her, a nun would make her hair stand on end, no, no, no, a
nun inspires confidence even in nonbelievers, a nun is a professional who suits a busy person, I saw the señora leaving for the
consulate, portfolios and lists of work to do, a nun is just like
she was, if you see her and have problems, you stop her in the
street and tell her and the nun brings her to us so she can direct
us, tell us what to do. No, a nun, but yes a nun, and at the end
they told me to come back tomorrow and we give you instruc-
tions but don't think about taking off the suit for from this
moment on you work for us and that's what you do until you
bring her to us

come back tomorrow

ready to work

come back tomorrow

at eight or seven thirty   better at six

women dressed as detectives

jazz singers

seamstresses

midwives

forensic doctors

economics students

we'll all come back

and I assure you that at least in my case I won't charge anything I have some savings and with what you're going to lend
me today

—And who told you we're going to lend you money? I don't
even know your name

—Analía

—I don't know but I imagine being blind like you are you
should have plenty of money and this is a cause that, well, really deserves it.

—Come on, sister, you know perfectly well I'm not blind.

—I'm not a sister either and yet

—it's not the same, either you can see or you can't

—but perhaps you're also not going around looking for
someone you can't find like everybody else?

don't you have that lost look that ignores people because
you don't see the person you'd like to see before you?

—Amazing how you understand, Analía.

—Pascual, save whatever you were going to spend on me for
coffee and give me a donation for the girls.

—Not now, I'm in a hurry. I believe I've found her.

—I'll go with you, I can't go back to my friends dressed like
I am and I don't know what to do until six in the morning.

125

—Don't think that between us

—Please, a blind man with a nun

—It wouldn't be bad. They won't be able to figure us out.

—Let me see your face, take off your headdress, I like to see a woman's hair, it's an image of her soul. Long. Short. Curly—straight or what's worse with a permanent.

—Stop joking. This is not a fashion show. Also you told me you were in a hurry. Admit that you're now forgetting about the woman you want to meet.

—That'll never happen.

—Till death do you part, is that it?

—If you only knew better I would not tell you. Certain things should be kept under wraps. In any case don't laugh, it brings back bad memories.

—For good reason your name is Italian. You don't find romantic men around here. Something in the food. Imagine their aim in life is to eat beef, drink red wine. Generations of men that down juicy steaks, in the end the only thing left to them is hair on the chest, a desire to take women to bed but words, memories, that no, that is something typical of Italians, Portuguese, Brazilians; Brazilians, mind you are in a class by themselves

—You've done a lot of research, sister.

—What does it matter to you since you don't even know me.

—No, I just said it, that's all.

—A pity.

—A pity?

—Nothing, I just said it, that's all.

live and let live

—If she's aiming at her temple it's because she wants to die.

—In front of so many witnesses it's more likely she just wants to make a scene.

—That's about it, yes. She'd like us to call the fire department, 911, an ambulance, offer smelling salts to her mother who's fainted. All that.

—Instead she has us. Indifferent but curious.

—To see such a show in the theater who knows how much we'd have to pay.

Analía was blond and slender. Everybody could see that, even when she was hidden beneath her nun's habit. Pascual Domenico Fracci hadn't failed to notice that she also had green eyes red nails and yellow teeth. *Smoker,* he said to himself, hiding his disgust with an artificial smile as he offered her his arm before ringing the bell of the *pensión. This way they'll open the door and let us in immediately. Nobody in this neighborhood distrusts pious women. What do they know?*

The one who opened the door was Hernán, the math teacher in Room B with a view of the garden.

—Excuse us. This is not a good time for visitors. We are extremely busy and have no time or money for donations. Don't look at me like that. The church has means, if you wish to collect money try the retirees, teachers, or poor devils from the circus next door who'll be deported any minute, separated from their children, lovers, and debtors. No. Today is absolutely not a good day for such things.

—You are mistaken, sir. Pascual Domenico Fracci at your service. I'm here to look for my fiancée because I'm sure she's in this house.

—A fiancée? In this house? Don't be funny, everyone here is now at the most intense point of a trial. There are no fiancées in this house. Bachelors, divorcées, widows, and women who don't care to talk about their past. But fiancées, well. Excuse me, sister.

Pascual Domenico Fracci knew she was there without seeing her, he closed his eyes and let his sense of smell guide him through the entryway while Hernán shocked by the kick he got smack on his left knee let himself be helped by Analía who offered him a swaying waist beneath the habit all things he used to appreciate very much during certain afternoons of his childhood of lubricious and melancholy altar boy. Juana didn't see him because her arm had begun to ache from holding the gun to her head the past three hours. The neighbors, crowded in the courtyard, were looking through the window but now bored with so much waiting lost her leap when Pascual let out a cry almost whimpered almost a serenade for a sweet-sixteen:

DOMINGUITA!!

Don't insist. She didn't dream of going dancing with him. She had lost the taste for his Piedmontese dishes, Spanish *cazuelas* had no more charm. Perhaps, as the newspapers would say later, she was mixed up and believed he was an assailant, the rapist of the poor nun who was running behind him with her habit awry and the blond mane escaping from the headdress. Don't insist. She didn't want people to call her that way and even though it's true she could have made that clear some other way through express mail or fax or e-mail since there it's like playing the lottery to try to send a letter or get through on the phone and any other methods lack the formality required of the written message, she whirled around immediately, looked him straight in the eyes, and fired.

shall I come with you?

Dr. Gutiérrez kept her shining, busied himself with the smallest details of her existence. He crooned to her at night, sang children's rounds and gave her kisses as sweet as birthday cakes. Massaged her, tickled her. Wanted to soften her. He was frightened by her glinting eyes that observed him in the darkness, the coldness of her breasts in early morning. To help her he had left his family and his practice. Nothing mattered to him. He was totally immersed in the mystery of his patient, his queen, the elusive girl with bad teeth who had grown a magnificent and inexplicable armor.

She is:
                    a stainless steel goddess
                              an
                        ex-kidnapped
                        ex-scarred girl
                          ex-leper
an ungrateful girl who does not call her kidnappers   an unbeliever who would forget him the minute they got back to the city   a calculating bitch   a nobody without a high school education   a frigid girl with a body like a tin can, a social climber who needs to go to the hairdresser, the siren of our dreams, the unattainable cipher of the doctor's love who now cannot cure her and lacking therapies offers bouquets of sleeping pills diet miraculous rejuvenating creams knowing she will reject them because she's into something else while he and we follow her absorbed asking her for a word, a signal, an order, the lash and breath of her power.

see what it's turned into?
just a piece of junk

Malvina dances in the midst of a swarm of mosquitoes and bees. She's barefoot and her feet sink into the floor covered by hearts of palm. The dance requires twisting, lifting the arms, then a somersault, pulling the short underarm hairs. It's difficult but Javier is ready to accompany her. She knows that for a man there's no rarer dish than a satisfied woman, crazy about life, a go-getter with no need of flattery or speeches. He dances and pants because Marta is now into something else. She has also found the face that waits for her at the bottom of her adding and subtracting and goes off with a family man to all the corners of his desire as if it were Sunday in an airport or a patriotic holiday in a country inhabited by men with dark skin and mustaches, blue shirts, shoes too highly polished.

They stop when Malvina falls into his arms and says *these mosquitoes are driving me crazy they keep biting me they don't let me live what can we do.* Now they'll never grow apart. Jail, business deals, investigation and closing of the cannery will only strengthen their love and for that love they will do everything necessary even that which everybody calls horrifying and that for them was the highest moment of their life. But let's not anticipate dangers because right now they're making love, rolling around on the floor, slipping on hearts of palm. Fury of salmonella. Urge for nutmeg and drops of honey. It's their wedding music. That's how we understand it even when we can only glimpse at their dreams.

Meanwhile Fran Camufa is preparing a devastating editorial that will sweep away any request for clemency. Fran Camufa defends:

1. The right to eat noncontaminated foods

2. The right to consume the produce from one's own garden

3. The persecution and imprisonment of any worker with dandruff, cold, or depression, conditions that endanger the honest and sanitary exercise of producers and consumers of food

Fran Camufa demands:

1. The return of the Scarred Girl
2. The investigation of the death of any person or persons who may have eaten the day before they expired

don't fuck around with me

SCIENTIFIC AND LITERARY NEWS

CORRELATION BETWEEN THE INGESTION OF FOODSTUFFS AND DEATH CONFIRMED BY SCIENTIFIC AND STATISTICAL SOURCES

AN INTERNATIONAL GROUP of scientists from the multinational force called by the Commission for the Defense of the Rights of the Eating Public has confirmed that virtually 99.5 percent of deaths have occurred 24 or even fewer hours after eating. The variety of diets of the cases studied, differences in age, and conditions of health in the examples that span a wide sample of the society suggest a close link between ingestion of foodstuffs and death. The banquet scheduled for the closing session has been postponed until further notice.

ᴵᴵᴵᴵᴵᴵᴵᴵᴵᴵᴵᴵᴵᴵᴵᴵᴵᴵᴵᴵᴵᴵᴵᴵᴵᴵᴵᴵ

YOUNG KIDNAPPED GIRL RECOVERS FROM LACERATIONS

IN A DEVELOPMENT described as miraculous the young girl who was tortured by her kidnappers reacted favorably last Sunday to her treatment. *Our prayers have been answered,* her mother stated, unable to hide her emotion before the congratulations offered by the head of the Republic. *Now we can only hope that other such unfortu-nate girls will have similar luck,* said the doctor on duty without offering any greater optimism.

ᴵᴵᴵᴵᴵᴵᴵᴵᴵᴵᴵᴵᴵᴵᴵᴵᴵᴵᴵᴵᴵᴵᴵᴵᴵᴵᴵᴵ

LIST OF VICTIMIZED GIRLS GROWS

ACCORDING TO UNOFFICIAL sources the number of girls scarred in incidents related to the disappearance of Miss Noemí, alias the Leper Girl, alias La Llagadita, has multiplied in the capital and in the northern provinces. The official number of 105 would be inconsistent with the figures released by local hospitals and the declarations of neighbors, which would increase the count to 546.2, thus including attempted cases of kidnappings.

ᴵᴵᴵᴵᴵᴵᴵᴵᴵᴵᴵᴵᴵᴵᴵᴵᴵᴵᴵᴵᴵᴵᴵᴵᴵᴵᴵᴵ

HE LIED ABOUT THE CHOLERA TO RID HIMSELF OF HIS DEBTORS

IN A SCHEME DESCRIBED as disgusting by those affected, Román Esteban Camporani, resident of the San Benedito district, summoned his debtors, asked them to put his loan documents on the floor, and, claiming to have cholera, defecated all over the papers.

Medics and the police were called to the scene and stated with certainty that the aforenamed is known for his tricks to avoid payment of his debts. This time he went too far, said the doorman of the apartment building where Camporani lived. The Ministry of Public Health assures the public that there is no danger of contagion.

hate to admit it but it hurts

Dear Diary:

Such a long time since we were alone. Dr. Gutiérrez doesn't leave my side from sunrise to sunset. Sometimes I believe I'm dreaming about him and I wake up to see him staring at me because he says he can't bear my sleeping with my eyes open. He's afraid of me since he discovered my scars were made of nylon. What's it to him, is what I say. But he insists, keeps searching for the secret that I won't tell him, he threatens to find the señoras and do things to them, put them on the grill because it seems he's one of those doctors that advise the police during interrogations. Yesterday when he cried he reminded me of a man who gave me tips just so he could talk to me about a daughter who'd gone abroad with a guy who put her out on the street to work. In a country where she didn't know the language, the evil of such people has no limits, poor girl. Dr. Gutiérrez has soft hands, I'm aware of it by how he moves them when he polishes me and lingers on the part where my breasts are. That's when you see him with a thread of saliva at the corners of his lips, and so what. He must be used to things as they were before. I don't let him know I notice because what could I offer to that gentleman as busy as I am with the training. Although I can tell you I'm beginning to like him and if he doesn't go over me with a soft cloth as he usually does I miss it. It'll heat you up like soup, that's what he says.

Yesterday I talked on the phone with the señoras and they told me it will be soon. I practice and practice. That smile they request will finally appear. I'm sure of it. The only misgiving I have is this matter of Dr. Gutiérrez. It seems essential that I escape within the next few days.

TODAY I FEEL ALMOST WELL. THE WOUND HAS OPENED ALL THE WARM FEELINGS OF MY HEART. BEFORE IT WAS AS THOUGH I HAD A BAD COLD AND NOW WITH THE AIR THAT ENTERED ME I CAN BREATHE BETTER, THEY PUT ME IN AN OXYGEN TENT AND I CAN FEEL LOVE, IT TICKLES WHERE I HAVE STITCHES. BUT, MY DEAREST, I MISS YOU.

FROM TIME TO TIME THEY GIVE ME NEWS OF YOU. THEY SAY YOU ARE DOING OK IN PRISON, THAT FROM ONE DAY TO THE NEXT SURPRISINGLY ENOUGH YOU RECOVERED YOUR HEIGHT AS A WOMAN AND STOPPED BEING A LITTLE GIRL. MIDGET, THE NURSE SAID. YOU WERE A MIDGET. I PAY NO ATTENTION TO HER. WHAT DO THEY KNOW ABOUT OUR AF-FAIRS? THEY SAY I'M NOT ALLOWED TO WITHDRAW THE COMPLAINT THEY BROUGHT IN THE CASE, THAT YOU COULD HAVE KILLED ME. THEY DON'T UNDERSTAND. THEY WILL NEVER UNDERSTAND THE URGE THAT MAKES ME SEEK YOU. OBVIOUSLY I FORGIVE YOU. I WOULD LIKE YOU TO COME TO SEE ME. NOW AND NOT WHEN I GET OUT. THEY SERVE A DISH OF CARROTS CUT VERY FINE AND STEAMED THAT YOU'LL LIKE. THEY NEVER CAME OUT THAT WAY FOR ME WHEN YOU ASKED FOR THEM AND NOW I HAVE THEM AND YOU'RE NOT HERE. MY LOVE. AMONG ALL WOMEN YOU'RE THE ONE I WAIT FOR, THE ONLY ONE WHOM I ALLOW ALL AND OF WHOM I ASK ALL.

YOURS,
PASCUAL DOMENICO FRACCI

(The paper smells of medicines and has splotches of disinfectant. No envelope because all the prisoners' correspondence has to be read before it's turned over to the recipient and before this letter reaches Juana it will be seen by three old spinsters, an illiterate corporal, and mistakenly by the office of the secretary of the Real Estate Board who, indignant at seeing the passion missing in his life, will go home and beat up his wife who will pack her bags the minute she recovers and go off to the circus where Marta has been waiting for her for months now because as you can imagine she needs someone to help her with the inventory now that she has sunk into the arms of a man who'll never understand.)

Let's be realistic

It's Sister Analía who visits him every day. I see her arrive with her nun's step like someone who's just stopped wearing high heels, the headdress balanced with some effort and I don't pity her, although when she turns around and looks at me she seems to be apologizing for her great interest, so many things she asks and keeps on asking until the poor guy begins to lose his breath or spit blood and we have to ask her to leave.

The sister begs him for information because she believes she's onto something. Yesterday she was talking to him about a prize, a payment. If it concerns redeeming that woman, what luck for her. Other women shoot once and rot in jail, but this one has two attempts to her credit and it seems she's being made a saint. I wait for her also because she had something familiar about her, an air that carried me back to other times and when I saw her expression in the newspaper photograph I felt an emptiness in the pit of my stomach and a wish to sun myself on the balcony of my house but now I can't do things like that because, well, people don't do such as that anymore, age, wrinkles, cancer, and so on.

I spied on her when she went to the bathroom and saw the garters and her black underwear. I saw her dab perfume between her breasts and later pull herself together, look serious, become again the little nun but once I knew about that bleached hair I couldn't get it out of my mind and now, I swear, when I walk along the street every nun seems to me to be hiding something. Yes, you're right, they'll say to me. But nobody knows anything about anybody; I always thought that beneath the headdress they had just a bit of limp hair. Limp. No spray. Or moisturizers. No color enhancement. But this one has all that, particularly when she leans over Señor Fracci's bed and says in a very soft voice *Pasquale, Pascualito, who is the woman who shot you? Wouldn't she perhaps be the one whose trail I've been following? Come on, Pascualito, don't pretend to me you're suffering from love since what you've got is a hole made by the bul-*

let of an angry woman. A woman who could help me in the search for the señora. Pascualito, say something to me and I'll help you, I'll bring her here so she can visit you, I'll get her out of prison. I'll guarantee her good behavior. No way is she your fiancée. She's a wild one and if you want my humble opinion you should be furious at her.

GET OUT OF HERE
CONNIVING HARPY
UNDERCOVER CREEP
SPY
LEAVE US IN PEACE
WE'RE HAPPY
WE LOVE EACH OTHER SHE HAS GIVEN ME HER FREEDOM I'M THE ONE SHE SHOT AND NOT JUST ANY OTHER MAN A STRANGER SHE WAS WAITING FOR ME

**GET OUT OF HERE
STOP MEDDLING
JEALOUS BITCH**

The shouts alerted the personnel. They came from all sides leaving their patients unfed half starved and now crowded in the hallways, disheartened for lack of a bed, wanting to try the carrots saved from the salmonella plague. Most were men because the women were used to dieting and for years skipping meals had become a sport for them, one they had to hide under various pretexts, *no, thanks just had a big breakfast finished an early lunch with a friend from the country*—they knew only too well that dieting made men wary, they'd immediately assume that such women lived in cold houses with no comforting smell of stew simmering away while they painted their toenails to make themselves more attractive after spending the day shopping for ingredients for an amazingly fragile dessert shaped like a tower, candle on top sporting a hat that ends in a chocolate cone topped by a maraschino cherry.

143

Pascual's chest hurt and hurt from the effort. Nurses, doctors, and even the kidnapper of the girl he returned to her parents five years later, who'd paid his debt to society by collecting bandages from private clinics and bringing them to the municipal hospital, joined them. He's going to die on us. What's his last wish, we must ask him. We have to grant him whatever he wants so we can sleep well at night so we won't be haunted by his screaming guts. Pencil and paper, he's almost gone—can no longer talk.

MY BEAUTIFUL MURDERESS

That was his wish. Written in his own hand. He gave us his request and we will fulfill it because there's nothing like death.

IV
Here there's not a soul that hasn't gone hungry

one by one you'll pay

—She was desperate. Like a madwoman.

—They brought her against her will, that's why she wanted to take off and if they hadn't grabbed her she would have escaped.

—Luckily it was the nun who turned her around.

—I think she must have threatened her with something.

—But what could a poor nun threaten her with. Humble soul who stopped eating like all of us, chaste, timorous, woman from convent and church. No. I think she stayed because she realized he needed her and she repented. She wanted him to forgive her.

—She probably recalled some time when he took her to a movie. No matter how many presents a man gives a woman, what she really likes is for him to take her to the movies. Something that implies commitment, to be seated there for two hours, sometimes longer if there are ads, to travel to other places through movies, be invited into houses and affairs by strangers, and later to come out, walk along a dimly lit street discuss the movie, say as for me it seems this way or that, what would you do in their place because for myself, once although it may seem like a fib I was in such and such situation, I liked that scene when it was foggy because in my house when I was a kid there was always fog or maybe it was a chemical cloud from the factory next door or from the dye plant across the street but fog always gives me the shivers I can't explain why then he already feels she's giving him something that memory and all because of the movie then there's a closeness between them and they can go to bed it's not like just going out to eat and later well you know without any respect or consideration   the movie dignifies everything   he has already shared feelings with her and when they're in bed they can hear the music of the movie that from that day on will make them remember the first time

—that's the way my first husband thought and put me

147

through one shameful situation after another with porn movies that he took me to see every Thursday afternoon

—don't talk like that he was a good man

—what do you know about it?

—You can tell. Remember the gusto with which he ate
everything you made for him even when you got that obsession of making that cold hearts of palm salad every day

—The thing is she wanted to escape but later looked at him
in such an odd way

—Luckily I remembered about the eyeglasses

—Even so, to him she gave the impression of having those
eyes drilling into him

—But he smiled, nearly done for and all he kept smiling

—He was happy because of the sister

—I don't think so. People about to die are like babies they
smile when they pass gas.

let her through,
the young lady is coming with me

In the rooms various games of chance and a single solution jump into the void   taciturn losers stand in line on a balcony leap down after posing in front of a camera and signing a document exonerating the casino from all responsibility   we live under a rule of law and it's not like it was before when each suicide happened at random without forms without leaving a trace or writing capricious and incomprehensible letters that complicated the arrangements of estate probates, registry of patents, testimonies of the egotism of people to a tremendous degree   without order   we live in a city aware of its own greatness and that's why a clear point is necessary, a logic to entering and exiting. You stand in line and wait your turn. In front of me is a man who's won a fortune and wants to give us ninety-nine point nine percent of it but nobody wants to lose their place in line if they do they'll have to go back and place bets   run risks   chat with the croupier   no no no we all know that his generosity is a sham and we say enough this is an inadmissible joke, a trick to deny us our vertigo   my time will be soon   I feel the aura of the square below   at the bottom and the impact of the red brick pavement on the neck, it's always the neck.

you've got to takc your chances

They were photographed looking boldly at the camera. She was smiling glistening proud of the row of aluminum teeth. He held his left hand between his legs, in the right a steaming spoon

THEY WERE HAVING SOUP
Caressing each other
SWALLOWING SO EVERYONE COULD SEE THEM
he had tartar on his gums

and not because they were hungry

None of that mass of frightened skeletons for me, enough fear of death. In love with the asymmetrical shadows of the stateless she went to the stadium where they'd been gathered and almost without looking found the ideal dining companion. She took him by the arm to the square and before the photographer served him a magnificent picnic. Together insolently looking at us in the eye their picture was in all the papers. Neither lovers nor engaged nor repressed neighbors. Just colleagues. A satisfied stateless man because for some time now all food was sent to the stadium. The people waited for the results of that diet, the death of the intruders that undoubtedly would come to the same sad end of all those who ate but the results were the opposite and the population grew. They multiplied at an incredible rate. They spoke languages with jarring sounds, communicated with each other with gestures and songs, had babies with sunflower faces, orange, gray, and green. Mixed together and created a linguistic pandemonium. Afternoons they enlivened the stadium with remarkable feats. Entire families swung on a toothpick, bet on mosquito races, yelled at their tame butterflies because nobody had forgotten that they formed part of an age-old circus. The stadium became a neighborhood. At times tourists arrived from the same countries of origin as the illegals and on discovering them turned their faces away and left in a hurry fearful of being recognized by someone capable of saying the word that would wreck their itineraries and bar them from cocktail parties they'd been asked to attend by those who put a high price on their exoticism. Meanwhile the population of the country was decimated. They were healthy slender corpses. Their diet gave them a disciplined grimace and they went to the other world with the satisfaction of an exercise well completed.

Malvina had started eating fresh hearts of palm because the tickles no longer pleased her and that was the only thing that gave her the shivers of moonlit nights. And at this moment, stylish guerrillera, she licks her lips with the man she'd kidnapped from the stadium and yakked and yakked with him in a coded language. I can tell you in all honesty that the little threads of saliva that curl from the corners of their lips don't bother me.

Have no doubt about it, this will be a scandal

(I have personally taken the photograph to be developed and I know it's been distributed to every daily newspaper in the city defying all dietetic and racial laws.)

Another imperialist provocation?

THE PHOTOGRAPHS THAT ARE currently being shown in our circles represent a desperate attempt to oppress us. Fearful of the forces that proclaim our independence, the henchmen of evil pretend that we ingest the poison of their soups and beverages. Let us resist the temptation, the free dinners in enemy restaurants, the snacks skillfully disguised as savory dishes, and understand they are cockroaches of the spirit, mirages meant to distance us from our free and martyred destiny.
Fran Camufa

||||||||||||||||||||||||||||||||||

Everybody knows it. They would eat until they choked and then put on a corset so nobody could see they'd broken the rules. And they weren't the only ones. The country had to create a black market of foreign currencies to mask the traffic of armor going on simultaneously in underwear, bullet-proof vests, and concealers of rolls of fat. Some became very rich and beat a noisy retreat bringing about traffic jams at airport entrances. At times one had to wait several hours in the car in the middle of a blazing sun but it was worth the trouble because the minute they got on the plane they could undo the corset and say with a sigh, now at last one can breathe.

The illegals were very amused at the whole thing because they were back again and blossoming pleased with choruses of farewell and a clandestine bank of advice for first-time travelers. They sent them to all the islands that did not require visas and they could immediately go to work buying and selling rumors to be transmitted late at night over the Internet.

a heart of gold

—The moment has arrived, I must go to be with my people.

—But for myself I like the beach very much, this is my dream come true. To watch the sea every day eating up the trash that people throw into it. A clean sweep. I spit something out in the afternoon and in two minutes it's off to Paris or to add to the meal of some fish I don't know about but the fact is I don't have it. So many years to heal, generate garbage of foreign bodies and now that I've found the best way to shed everything, you want to go.

—But who said we have to go together? I'm ready to leave by myself.

—I love you, I saw the scars, I helped you. It's not fair.

—And you love all your patients like that? And those you fried with the electric prod also?

—They've been telling you rumors

they've been filling your head with ancient history   events of a generation of old retired hopeless men and women pains in the ass disappeared in the city's smoke who didn't even know the simplest facts about their friends

they've been lecturing you so you would despise and discredit me I who work for nothing

I'm the one who does everything possible so the snot
doesn't ruin your aluminum

that's the way you thank me

sneak

distrustful

anorexic and all   you have the gall to complain and denounce me

in this city they don't let up it's no longer enough to have a university degree and to open the wallet

now they want retroactive generosity   where were they when the loot was divided up when we passed out the bribes   I'll bet you they were waiting in line   and you disguised as a leper

what could you have been up to   why are you coming to me
with those things

  —When you come with me you won't be able to talk so
much.

  —you're taking me?

  —as attending physician but totally in secret

  —journalists don't tread where ants go.

baby, scratch my eyes out if you like

He took her hand and she in handcuffs couldn't smile at him because Analía had recognized her. She realized that the sneer corresponded to goings and comings, chases, love affairs, and business carried out in a doorway. She saw her bend toward Pascual Domenico Fracci and felt her spit a second before she let it out, exact, wounding, with a round green ball of gum on the tip. The nurses got heartburn from shock because since they'd begun eating only two days before everything affected their digestion. One wanted to give her a slap but her hand was so greasy from pizza that Juana thought it was a caress and licked it with such loving impudence that Pascual Domenico Fracci, drowning in the spit that had landed inside his nostrils, trembled with the voluptuousness of a newlywed.

My dears:

DON'T HAVE THE SLIGHTEST DOUBT

Pascual Domenico Fracci has died. Drowned but happy. Shipwrecked in Juana's scorn. You will say:

a woman with no sense   out of her mind   nuts

a murderess

an unfortunate daughter who keeps her mother with her heart in her mouth

a crazy woman who stretches and shrinks like a cheap sweater but I know her and know she's also lost something and now she looks at us from the newspaper photograph

MURDERESS UNMOVED
BY THE DEATH OF THE VICTIM

I see her as the girls of the Eva cult will see her and the apples appear because I recognize her and will follow her anywhere as usual, above all when the mother, basket in hand, manages to help her escape from jail. But before, as you might imagine:

    1. They took her back to the police station.

    2. She was besieged by journalists.

3. Analía pinched her ass to see if it was truly as hard as it looked.

4. She started singing SHAMELESSLY a ditty that rhymed with *impetigo* and naturally set off a wanton wailing among all the paparazzi milling around her.

5. She became virtually a millionaire from the offers that poured in from all sides. In Peru they called her the *belle dame sans merci* and in some cities that I won't mention for obvious reasons they awaited her liberation with leather gadgets, chains, black jackets and felt animals for the little girls abused by the elementary school teachers.

6. Analía decided to put on nail polish and bleach her hair blond.

now don't look at me like that
don't any of you understand anything?
(*they've been so good and quiet*
that she lets them come into the dressing rooms)

—First thing is the mask. I'll put it on you. And a hood.

—Oh, no. None of that. I'm going this way.

—But don't you see they're going to recognize you and you're not going to be able to make a statement in time? You're going to have half the country hanging on your every movement. They're not going to let you through, Malvina. They're all the ones who can no longer put up with the corsets, colic, hunger, the secret. They've had it and are going to look to you for a solution.

—You're totally mistaken. They'll think I'm coming dressed as a torturer and they'll let me have it with all they've got. This business of the mask is too compromising. On the other hand it may be an advantage, gives the aura of another time. False eyelashes and perhaps a fur coat so they don't notice my welts. If they do see them they'll think they're due to the salmonella. A fur coat is very good for a woman in my situation. It makes people think of bribes, the possibility of a cushy job. You get better service.

—But with this hot weather they'll think you're nuts.

—Well as for you, you'd better concentrate on your pronunciation. Nobody's interested in a foreign lawyer. Pick easy words, nothing to do with the circus, nothing that might make them catch on that you're a clown, a stateless person born by chance in a tent, smelly, with an elephant snout and the face of a hardtack biscuit.

—Don't start in or I'll serve you hearts of palm.

—Don't keep it up baby can't get away from me and you know it.

⁓

—The aluminum has to be very shiny.

—It looks better a little dark. It lends class. Think of the Metropolitan Museum in New York, for example, does the medieval armor shine? No, because it has the authenticity of years, and the people are fascinated and go to look at it, but how are you going to remember, poor girl, if you've never gone anywhere, I'm sure no one ever took you, lack of wherewithal, or interest.

—That's enough because I'm getting bored, now polish it well so it looks like a mirror.

—Like a mirror?

—So when they look at me they'll see themselves. A mirror. It enlarges. Let them see, let them get a body wax and makeup.

꘎

The body of Pascual Domenico Fracci is tiny. They put it in a package and sent it parcel post to his children. The grandchildren he never knew mill around and ask their parents to open the present but one daughter-in-law smells trouble, writes FOR EXPORT, and sends it to the Eva Cult Foundation so they'll let her alone finally. We believe the ploy worked because the postman who left it at the door swears that after two days there was no more odor of death in the street. *Those girls are something from another world. There isn't a problem they don't know how to solve.* Now that they're about to fulfill their obligations everybody in the neighborhood loves them. The premenstrual festivals have been incorporated into the rhythm of the city. Dressed in red, men, postmenopausal women, children, and lost teenagers celebrate their fears and whims accompanying them with their ballyhoo and signs through the streets in demonstrations larger and racier all the time.

francesita que trajiste pizpireta,
sentimental y coqueta . . .
(don't you love imports?)

As was to be expected she arrived in a Concorde and the very moment of landing at the airport she demanded that the pilot be given the weekend off so they could go to nightclubs, have fun, and get drunk before taking a shower together in the most luxurious hotel and going to sleep in a bed with satin sheets that matched the violet-colored roses they'd put all over to welcome her. She shouted all this because it was essential for them to understand that here was a woman of definite appetites, a hot, tough piece of work. What are you going to do, she said to the pilot, *this is underdevelopment for you. You have to become famous. Show them what you're capable of if you don't want to be eaten alive.* What a fuss for a news story. What a to-do so they'd let her see Juana.

The other women had been sent by agencies who'd invested too little in the enterprise. They wore tailored suits, used cheap deodorants that left white spots on their polyester blouses and nights they smoked and shouted at each other from the little balconies of cheap hotels, in bathrobes and hair curlers. It was easy to see they had no spunk, nothing in their favor, but they believed some guy or other would fill the void and told each other stories of this pickup and that sweetheart. Of the forty-five who arrived, two were shipped back in a hurry because foreign adulterous women are not tolerated; one became a nun and too late founded the convent that could have taken in the other two; another had the sickness but was able to hide it until she was seventy-five years old; three went to work for Marta who at that stage of the game had turned herself into a character—she wore dark glasses, always dressed in black and was expert in the import-export business, after having been impregnated by undocumented workers in unions resulting in children the color of the rainbow, and the rest persisted, played hopeless tricks on our slated-for-success French journalist, suffered humiliation. Made plays for the pilot and were rejected, who anyway was desperately in love with the Concorde mechanic. The French journalist had everything she needed to guarantee her fame and when Juana agreed to the interview she entered the prison like the star she is.

once there were two hearts
that beat as one . . .

UNPUBLISHED REVELATIONS ABOUT THE BRUTAL MURDERESS

EXCLUSIVE INTERVIEW
FOR *POLITICS AND SOCIETY*
BY OUR SPECIAL
CORRESPONDENT
CHANTAL DES MESNAIRS

On a gray rainy afternoon the efforts of several months were rewarded and I found myself face to face with the so-called brutal murderess in an inhospitable cell of the Women's Prison that also houses the frigid, the orphaned, and the indigent. We talked for two hours while the murderess ate ravenously lettuce leaves brought in by a volunteer named Sister Analia who has accompanied her throughout her captivity.

—There's been much talk about your changes in size. Are they caused by a special diet? Our national and international readers would like to know the origin of these transformations and for you to clarify the question of all those products that use your name in their advertising.

—There are things in life that are inexplicable. For me love has transforming power. That's all I can say in this regard for the moment.

—Love? You? Everybody knows you killed poor Pascual Domenico Fracci in cold blood. And afterward you grew so much that a hole had to be made in the ceiling in order to get you out of the hospital. Is it love that made you swell up so the buttons popped off your blouse? Don't you think our readers will find your response difficult to believe?

—Pascual Domenico Fracci is, has been, and will be the great love of my life. It doesn't matter whether people understand or accept it.* I don't pretend that you can even guess at all the ties that bind us but it is for his sake that I accept my imprisonment since you know very well I have more than sufficient means to get out of this dog kennel, you're surely not going to believe that this display of guards and wardens is anything more than a parade of beggars waiting to be of service. I am, after all, a woman who can pay for her transfers without any trouble.

—Your mother defends you despite the accusations you made against her in a legal suit concerning the alleged poisoning of your father . . .

—My mother will be judged with the rest of the country in the hearts of palm scandal; her defending me doesn't change anything. She cannot justify her behavior. She is a low, immoral person. Like many women she doesn't realize that what I did openly is an act of infinite love. Don't you see the difference with the case of the hearts of palm? Pascual knew the degree to which I've been and will be faithful to the resentments that bring us together. Pascual was a man of imagination capable of

---

*NOTE OF EYEWITNESSES: At that moment she gets agitated, wants to take off her clothes, her right arm begins to grow. Sister Analía assures us that she is having a seizure, screens her, sings to her, and manages to calm her down. Even though the right arm shrinks, and the left increased in size and to almost its length. Our suggestion to use a tape measure was vigorously rejected by the alleged criminal and her companion. (*The complete text of the interview will be published in the* Daily Life *magazine of our Sunday edition. Don't miss it.*)

169

dying for love and I provided him with a form to contain our passion, that's why he kept smiling at me until the fatal spit.

—However, his children blame you now for breaking up their home and it wasn't just any home: the abode of hardworking immigrants who hardly had a minute free and did not indulge in making love without rhyme or reason or go around in telephone booths taking off their underclothes and scandalizing the neighbors but who procreated, continued the species, contributed to society.

—And do you have children? That very tight suit certainly wouldn't fit you so well if you'd given birth to twins or one of those chubby babies in the ads, a seven-month baby perhaps, but that involves other risks, I bet people would notice the circles under your eyes. Give me a break. My dear Chantal, so much contributing to society leaves its tracks.

now you see it
now you don't

Fran Camufa has nothing to say now. She's been dissolved, separated, once again become two unlucky colleagues packing their bags to go to the beach. They're changed. Aware of the competition. That freaky Juana, social climber with her cult and her companion, the fake nun, have begun to be idolized. All their plans, investment, pedagogy, the editorials written with so much effort to the point where they forgot they'd originally taken political positions to defend, had been of no use. Empty. Out in the cold. They work, strive. Go and return. Examine their notes and prepare to visit Noemí, the girl of the future. But for them

NADA

one of these days they'll go rummaging around in a shop. They'll have to buy themselves black velvet dresses to attend a presidential inauguration but at the last minute they'll realize that the invitations have not arrived, and all confused they'll wait at the door not knowing they'll get thrown out along with the greengrocer, the nurses from the hospital, and some young women journalists from upcountry who during the night of frustrations between whispers and caresses will uncover the secret find out why they went after one another play hide-and-seek and say good-bye suddenly to sweethearts with acne covered by a dollop of makeup snatched from their mothers' cosmetic case.

why do I love you so much? you tell me

—vitamins

—that's how I always was

—don't tell me that, plastic wounds and now that magnificent aluminum body

—vitamins, I tell you, dear, careful, abnegation

—beware of exaggerations

I am the armored woman

the self-taught

the rescued flea

my own fucking mother

BEWARE OF EXAGGERATIONS

nobody will say there were prescriptions doctors pedicures careful careful about exaggerating or showing common sense   now nobody will be able to undress me

every time they look at me:

tiny mirror

every time the curious would like to undress me:

they'll

see the writing on the wall

BEWARE OF EXAGGERATIONS

this is a romance with a taste of eternity   an engagement of each one with oneself   we'll dance all our lives   let's not talk about vitamins   shut your mouth   nobody has seen the past or knows I polish myself day and night   my shine is a secret   a sequin   the luminous spit of a famous sick man

—I'm going to blackmail you

—I'm going to pay you an astronomical salary

—I'll plot with the young girls who were raped to overthrow you

—he'll inject me with vitamins at night when no journalists or international dignitaries are around.

—and one of the girls will poison the syringe but then it'll
be too late

    —incredible how it gets late so early this time of the year.

did I tell you I saw him
with another woman?

The children of Pascual Domenico Fracci were neither idiots nor hermits. They turned up at the prison right away to see Juana with the proposal that they join forces in a campaign to have the body returned to the soil of the city that had been the birthplace of their love. Fracci's wife had changed her name after catching on one afternoon that her husband had left her. She remembered feeling a certain anxiety when she saw the anaesthesiologist who had attended her the next to last time she gave birth. *That man is onto something* she said to herself before being dragged toward a faded vision in which a kangaroo with false eyelashes was bowing regally before a woman who was selling counterfeit lottery tickets. The kangaroo knew they were worthless but bought them with expired bonds so the woman would believe she'd gained a fortune at his expense and would smile at him showing her red insolent gums. An exquisite romance was going on between the woman and the kangaroo, they massaged each other with their eyes and penetrated each other without ever touching until the inspector came by asking for documents. Impossible for the kangaroo: he had a pocket but was missing the consulate's seal; impossible for the woman because she was stateless. *That man is onto something.* He was the one whose documents the inspector wanted to see. He was the one and not Juana in the hospital and even less now in prison where she spies and sees how her children in chorus say: *No, our mother will not make any problem about our reclaiming the body; she left; she's nuts; probably doesn't even know her own name. Poor thing, getting old is terrible. Don't worry about it.*

As you might imagine, Salomé Moskovich the ex-Sra. de Fracci became an implacable enemy from that moment on. She bristled with schemes, her calendar bulged with tasks to be done

      banana peels on pedestrian walkways

                       anonymous letters

a bomb in the form of a peace dove given as a birthday present by a boy recently arrived from the countryside who would also ask for an autograph and then they'd die together because the bomb would explode in his hands just as he was handing her a fountain pen but for that she'd have to search for her date of birth and neither Juana nor her mother wanted it to get around oh Salomé ex-Sra. de Fracci   her vengeance her resentment her hatred sustained Juana's power, made her grow, surrounded her with the same intensity as waves of love offered by the girls of the Eva cult headed by Analía dressed as an airline hostess who hands out emblems bought with the reward for her discovery.

it pains me to admit it

Dear Diary:

I realized how shy he was when I smelled his shit. Like a kid. And he'd struck a match in the bathroom because he felt ashamed. Also the business of the cookies he keeps under his bed. At night he eats things shaped like trains, horses, chess pieces. Today I'll tell him and tomorrow we leave. I think if I hide his pants and make him agree to accept the deal wearing shorts it will be better. Here's hoping the señoras are still where they write their editorials it will make me feel weird to cast them aside, dear diary, after the pipe dreams they fed me. Fools.

cash only / no credit given here

—Chantal like *chantapufi*, unreliable, that's what we say here to liars. Naturally I'm not referring to you. A journalist of international fame, a professional whose integrity no one would doubt until well   someone plants a doubt. Above all now with the discovery of the business of Fran Camufa. Imagine keeping it hidden so successfully for almost a year.

—That Fran Camufa is a phenomenon typical of a third-rank country. Impossible in a developed country. We would have our spies, our well-tried infallible methods to ferret out the truth. One person who is actually two would never survive in that climate; she would have been followed by cameras hidden in street lights, through telephone taps. This is a well-protected society and not one like yours with police who are failed electricians, poking their electric prods here there and everywhere, totally at random. Wannabe machos in search of a quick erection. Law of the cocky prick. You won't get anywhere that way.

—Good, now let's get to the heart of the matter. Let's pick a date.

—But Analía, you must think it over carefully. Your life is here with Juana. There's nothing for you in France. You don't even know the language. And on top of that, there's the problem of a visa.

—Juana will come to find me when she gets tired of all this. Look at her now how she's sleeping. The hotel bed fits her perfectly right now. Let's hope her dreams don't bring her any fantasies of growing larger. She's just right this way. In a couple of days the judges will rule in her favor and then retire to the Caribbean with the money she gave them. Don't start in on stories about visas because I know everything will work out, particularly with someone as influential as you are.

—Don't overestimate the flexibility of the government and its employees. In the embassy there are people who cannot be bought, men and women happy to do the right thing, to go to modest cocktail parties and to receive exotic calendars from other employees in identical positions stationed in remote areas. The souvenirs are passed on to their children to console them for the frequent moves they have to make and the usual lack of playmates. No, your plans rely on suppositions that . . .

—how much would you charge me? I ask because I expect a price adjustment considering the embarrassment it would cause you if I reported that Juana never said a word after the first part of the interview and that I, generously but forced by you holding a pistol in your hand, was obliged to imitate the voice of the ferocious murderess for the tape recorder and to read the text that had already been prepared. It's unusual. Is it imported? Did you bring it directly from France?

—Certainly not. Analía, a woman must have a little foresight. Hollywood style. We discussed it for months with the team in charge of the video version and I as a Frenchwoman have only my name listed but you here don't understand anything being so far off the beaten track as you are, so you see the matter of the visa and all that is a daydream.

—Daydream is what you have. This pistol is a real one and Juana knows how to use it very well, and I'm her best student. Visa or not, I am your carry-on luggage so get used to the idea that I collect my debts from everybody.

better leave women alone,
you know how it goes
de las mujeres mejor no hay que hablar

—The price we agreed on was different.

—That was not a price. It was a deposit so that I would guard the goods while you clarify your situation about the visa and other matters.

—This is a scandal. You've swindled us. You've pushed your way into our lives while we were dancing, cooking our typical dishes, screwing by the light of the moon.

It had come to this. Beaten. Marta cornered. Her lover smiling. And the children all fired up to stone her when Analía arrived, out of breath, to obtain the necessary documents, accompanied by Chantal. It was late

It was anachronistic

The illegals had what they needed. The entire city, starving, had forgotten about the papers that divided them and now, gates open, files exposed, all the inhabitants fell upon the property records that Marta had stopped classifying years ago. Only the old people knew what they had owned and demanded that a certain box, a certain birth certificate be returned to them but the younger ones took the requests to mean such things were valuable and rushed forward, grabbing whatever they wanted to sell later in the chains of antique stores that would undoubtedly spring up in the neighborhoods that hordes of tourists would flock to attracted by the publicity about the long abstinence from food that had swept away a large part of the population.

What luck that Chantal was there

They recognized her and tamely began to form a line. All of them wanted to be interviewed. Some were hopeful of signing movie contracts, others were sure that with an interviewer of such scope they'd succeed in recognizing their destiny through questions wisely directed to them since up to that point few had clear goals in mind, clear ideas of why they'd started on their journeys. Famous for their exoticism but without first or last names since to pronounce them correctly was difficult for the native population only used to the art of country and folk music with crystal clear vowels, didn't want to lose the chance that a sophisticated European woman, educated in a Swiss boarding school for sure and lover of various diplomats and heads of state, would call them by their complete name and would write it in her article with no spelling mistakes and with all the consonants, circumflex accents, and umlauts correctly placed. Chantal moved forward, hieratic, regal, smiling, white white teeth. For all of them she still had the aura of the Concorde when she walked, the grace of keeping her balance while going to the bathroom in a plane experiencing turbulence. There was a journalist who could handle any crisis and later in a hotel kick back with a male for the occasion well dressed or not who cared she certainly didn't   an independent woman of the new world economy   a woman with plenty in her own bank account   a woman who could follow her own whims.

The immigrants wanted to attract her attention and standing before the table Chantal had improvised as a desk told her:

that they weren't immigrants but exiles

that during the revolution in their countries of origin all their property had been confiscated and they'd been revolutionaries who redistributed wealth only to be betrayed later by their lieutenants   more than that all the girls had been raped while very young some in the clinic when they were born and carried the indelible mark of aggression on their foreheads mothers by chance   sailors from ships that sank in unknown seas and that offered an alternative map of the earth   a police inspector while poking in Marta's files had found the person guilty of arson in the case of the library of Alexandria and now everybody wanted to crucify her according to an ancient journalistic custom of including some act of ritual violence in the front-page news and they would have done it if the atmosphere hadn't become suddenly charged with a persistent greasy smell that came in between legs and armpits preventing them from reasoning, smearing their words with something that simply made tongues heavy and put a drawl in their syllables.

It was, you guessed it, the powerful odor of rape

Some people, the most sensitive ones, had been perceiving it for months. It came from a corner of the garden where the acrobats had made a cave so they could sleep far from heights when they retired, abandoned and forgotten by everyone until that day, due to the breakdown of the social security system of the country that had completely abolished retirement, with no appeal, and naturally the acrobats fell like flies the minute one got Parkinson's disease or paused to pick his nose.

It was, my friends, a powerful odor of rape that had for some time been causing mothers to worry and daughters to feel a guilty fearful pang. Because of it the old goats had become bolder at the end of the school day, because of it tulips grew in the telephone booth, more than one girl felt an extraordinary itch run through her whole body and because of it, without re-alizing it, nuns in the convents wept overwhelmed by child-hood memories. There they were. The girls of the Eva cult. In the cave. And Chantal was left openmouthed for the very first time.

last tango, at least with you

LATEST NEWS

DR. GUTIÉRREZ REAPPEARS WITH MISS NOEMÍ

SOURCES IN THE CAPITAL reported that Dr. Gutiérrez and Miss Noemí, alias the Scarred Girl, La Llagadita, have been found in a seaside resort in the south. A press conference has been announced for today in which sources assure the mystery of his flight will be revealed.

‖‖‖‖‖‖‖‖‖‖‖‖‖‖‖‖‖‖‖‖‖‖‖‖‖‖‖‖

JUDGE RICARDONI RULES ERRONEOUSLY IN THE CASE OF THE COLDBLOODED MURDERESS

SEÑORA JUANA DEL CARPIO has been found not guilty in the case of the death of Pascual Domenico Fracci. The mistaken application of the law protecting the mentally ill was given as reason for the technical acquittal of the coldblooded murderess, now free to go

back into society. Surrounded by a group of faithful followers carrying apples held high she headed for a mansion rented especially by her mother allegedly with funds provided by the film production company that has secured film rights for the story. The mother confirmed to our special correspondent Chantal Des Mesnairs that she will not use the straitjacket suggested by Judge Ricardoni. *That judge must not ever have had children* she remarked to one of the boarders interviewed while she was packing her bags before leaving for the mansion.

‖‖‖‖‖‖‖‖‖‖‖‖‖‖‖‖‖‖‖‖‖‖‖‖‖‖‖‖

INTENSIVE THERAPY FOR NEW CASES OF SALMONELLA AND BOTULISM

A NEW OUTBREAK of salmonella and botulism is causing overcrowding in hospitals and clinics around the country. However, a return to the fasting that decimated the population is not recommended.

Say what you like the one who knows her best is Salomé and knows she can't stand her. With or without hat, inside or outside the telephone booth. To hell with her, she'd like to debunk the story, get herself into her own movie, win over Chantal, convince her that she indeed knows who Pascual Domenico Fracci was. But since she's erased all trace of her past life and doesn't care to be recognized by her children the only alternative left to her is to see if she can arrange something with the girls of the cult, the rape victims, the sweet-smelling teenagers with a record that could put any guy in jail that walks around hiding his fly with a checked jacket or the ubiquitous green beige raincoat. Salomé had established a school of dance entirely dedicated to various regional folk dances now that the stateless, free to work at whatever they wished, party and party without noticing that Salomé is charging tourists as well as locals an entrance fee so they can imitate and learn the dances. *Joy is contagious, the only sure way to learn,* she said to her clients who remember all her jokes and dance like crazy for the hour and forty-five minutes of each class. Salomé was getting ready for that when Noemí, the implacable, armored maiden, appeared first in the secret publication of the Army and later in children's magazines.

Reloj, detén tu camino . . .
can't bear to see her leave

Look at her. She's in the center. Men in uniform left and right. Generals. Admirals. Police officials. In a corner, Dr. Gutiérrez with hat and cane. If we didn't know him already from the newspapers we might not be able to see him, hidden as he is by the crowd in front. Her body is gleaming. The photograph exudes silence. We thought a cat had walked in front of the camera because you could see small footprints on the red and green arabesque design of the rug. Behind the group is the table where decrees will be signed and on the mahogany chest the marble pedestal to carry her through parks and cemeteries. Watch her with the diamond ring Dr. Gutiérrez gave her. See how it sparkles as if winking from her metallic finger. She is wanting to say good-bye or hi or see you later or nevermore. Today her eyes are fixed on us with a hard stare but the smile gleams, throws sparks, vapors of perfect breath, taste of mint. She is, we know, our fairy godmother.

I like high heels because they make
your ankles look slimmer

They're dancing an intoxicating tango. The blind accordionist plays and plays as if he were talking to himself. They're wearing their hair in a bun tight black dresses slit on the side. Cheap but not secondhand. Their legs touch, stay in place for a *sentada* make a lascivious figure eight, *un ocho,* undone as Juana obeys and lets herself be carried toward the other side of the salón while Chantal whispers in her ear: *come, come, let me introduce you.* The girls of the cult have recognized her because she still has a slight tic in the left eye. Besides they're tired and don't want to keep searching. Analía's schemes have now put them on bad terms with a whole series of biographical controls that have naturally revealed humble stories appearances of the virgin on flat roofs of adobe houses with clothes hanging on the line, sinful games with cousins of both sexes during the siesta, some illegitimate child sold to a family of gypsies posing as Swiss bankers, the shame of that night spent with a distant relative who left a card behind that said DR. GUTIÉRREZ, MEDICAL CLINIC and a doll whose value was that it was cross-eyed. Yes, the girls are tired, the reason they didn't even ask her name or demand passwords. Huddled together spoon fashion they simply chorused

PLEASED TO MEET YOU

and fell asleep like lambs in her shadow   in Juana's long enormous shadow

JUANA APPLE EATER

JUANA EX-MIDGET

All this gave the blind accordionist a tactile disgust, an intuition of emptiness among blue glitter in a space filled with whispers secrets taunts unfinished voyages that rose in his throat, and luckily, he manages to do what was necessary. Guided by his sense of smell he goes toward the cave now without the girls of the cult and settles down in the aroma of rape, drawn by the flower of his double and triple unconnected virtues. Because now, as you can hear, his voice is loud and clear. Now he sings like nobody else.

all or nothing at all . . .

—I know him better than anybody. I was his wife, I gave him the only children he ever had.

—But his alleged children do not recognize you. They say they have nothing to do with anybody named Salomé Moskovich, much less with a folk dance instructor. Isn't that proof enough that you are an impostor? How many lies do you think the people of this country are willing to accept?

—It doesn't surprise me that they don't recognize me, poor things. They always saw me in profile as I was cooking pasta, steak, meatballs. Amazing the dishes I made for them, including Pascual, of course. They gobbled up what I cooked for them right away and didn't need to look at me, say thank you, give me a kiss, they knew I didn't go in for flirtation, egotism, at that time, clearly. After the meal came the routine of washing the dishes, cleaning the kitchen, and going to work in the shop. Do you think they had time or reason to say to themselves *Now I'm going to look at my mama*? Do you think that would be healthy in boys concerned by what really matters? School, the university, soccer, make a career, find a sweetheart. I don't know what you believed but I'm not one of those women who put themselves in the forefront. For me the main thing always was that they were normal, ate well, had a nice sweetheart and there you see them. All settled.

—Yes, but now they don't even want to come visit you in prison. They say they are Juana's adopted sons and ask for the maximum penalty for your attempt to poison her. How did you get the idea of the hearts of palm? Do you know the charges made against Juana's mother? Look, it's really cruel to show her a can with the label so clear, serve her a quiche right in the middle of the demonstration against the BEAUTIFUL ARMORED GIRL. Now she's been left all shrunken, the size of a bride on a wedding cake.

—Don't make me laugh. The wedding cake figures are the girls of the cult that I don't know why the shit . . . excuse me, but it gives me such a feeling I can't describe seeing them with those rotten apples. I would like you to send this article to all the newspapers abroad so a campaign can be organized to recover the remains of my deceased, my Pascual Domenico Fracci. My beloved, adored husband, so vilely assassinated.

—I don't think that pose will look good in the photo. When you say vilely bite your lip a little so that a bit of blood trickles down, it will make a big impression on the public. Blood always sells well.

—And can't you do it with ketchup? I could hold a bit in my mouth and that way it would seem even redder, I don't want to get my lips infected, just redden the corners. Later I'll look like one of those teenagers with herpes. They take on the airs of femmes fatales with those red spots. Young people, I tell you.

—Ah don't sound like an old woman, nobody likes that. Even if they know you had all those children and spent so many boring years of life in conjugal bliss, you should seem younger. I don't care about the herpes business, I want you to bite your lip so your face shows a sorrowful expression. Allow me to ask you a personal question, just out of curiosity. Did you love the deceased?

—Look. Professional privilege I believe they call it. Now you're asking reporters' questions. And here I thought we were just having a friendly chat.

heart

Dear Diary:

My eyelids hurt but I'm delighted that people speak to me in the street and carry me on their shoulders. Today was my birthday and they gave me a lovely doll that talks and says: *my name is Juanita.* Dr. Gutiérrez really wanted to share it with me but I wouldn't let him; after all it's mine and the people will be impressed when they see me with it on the balcony. What I want is for them to remember when they were kids and wanted to have a doll like mine. She is the deepest secret of my reign: they mustn't know that she really eats, has fits of diarrhea when I give her watermelon with water and we get drunk together with champagne left over after military parades. They mustn't know, dear diary, because they're going to take her away from me and put her in my museum. They think I'm not aware of it but I know they're making plans and I even saw my showcase. As for Dr. Gutiérrez I forgive him all the dirty tricks; at bottom he loves me and that's why I'd like him to be the one to look me over and arrange everything when they make me into a statue. He certainly knows what suits me, what products to use to polish my armor. Not like the señoras with that stupid business with the scars.

by bike

The messenger had come by bicycle from China. Not exactly next door. It was night when he arrived in the city. The
streets were slippery because rain had been falling for the entire
week but the instant he set foot in the country the sky cleared,
the electricity came back on, and everyone began to go outside, blinded by the lights of show windows and the neon signs
that had been off for a month. The stateless people pinned on
emblems from mixed up uniforms they'd won in the lottery
organized by Malvina in hopes of collecting funds to defend
themselves in the international courts of justice; the girls of the
cult were red-faced because of the excessive exercise to get
ready for the championship soccer match organized by the Armored Girl in these the most difficult moments in her exercise
of power; the groups of teenagers, snatched from slow mastur-
bation siestas in their darkened rooms, went through the
streets with intimate smiles, ready to go to bed with the newly
arrived guy or any one of his future female assistants; Salomé
Moskovitz wasn't there because she'd received an invitation
from the recently established government of a country with no
past that required her services to establish a program of ances-
tral dances and typical dishes; Marta, Sra. del Carpio, the
nurses, the prisoners, and the sick from the time of the hearts
of palm were in the first row.

The boy gets down from his bicycle. A circle has formed
around him. Despite the fact that Chantal tries to elbow her
way to where she can look directly at the camera, we can only
see the package that contains the body of Pascual Domenico
Fracci and Juana who comes forward, dressed as an odalisque,
small but unmistakable, to undo the first knot.

(to be continued)

About the Translation

All Night Movie is a novel embedded in popular culture and the media. Although it takes place in an imaginary city, the Latin American context is clearly evoked in its language and rhythm. We have left fragments of song lyrics in Spanish when we felt they could be easily identified by readers. One example is the case of "Muñequita Linda," popularized by Nat King Cole singing in Spanish with a heavy North American accent. It becomes "*Muñequita linda /* my own little Goldilocks," with the English phrase added to bring out the meaning and feel of the original. Whenever we kept some Spanish, we provided an equivalent word or phrase in English that would indicate meaning as well as level of language and emotional coloration of the original.

In most cases we translated everything, even if it meant explaining tango lyrics. Some are translated freely without a reference to the musical piece, as in "*esto que hoy es un cascajo,*" which becomes "see what it's turned into? just a piece of junk." Our aim was to preserve the easy flow and chatty rhythm of the original. We enjoyed playing with the "inbetweenness" of the two languages to produce a translation that would render as accurately as possible the tone, irony, and sheer energy of the Spanish.

The rapid incorporation of Spanish vocabulary and popular culture into the mainstream of the English-speaking world leads us to believe that English readers may find pleasure in hearing the ring of Spanish in our English text.

About the Author

Alicia Borinsky, winner of the 1996 Latino Literature Award for Fiction, is a poet, novelist, and literary critic who writes in both English and Spanish. Her books include the novels *Mean Woman* and *Dreams of the Abandoned Seducer,* the poetry collections *The Collapsible Couple* and *Timorous Women,* and a volume of literary criticism, *Theoretical Fables: The Pedagogical Dream in Contemporary Latin American Fiction.* She is a professor of Latin American and comparative literature at Boston University.

To receive a reader's guide for this title contact the publisher:

Reader's Guide
Northwestern University Press
625 Colfax St.
Evanston, IL 60208
nupress@northwestern.edu

Please allow two weeks to process your request.